PILOT ERROR

PILOT ERROR

Harry Dale

Foreword by
E. Hubbard

The Book Guild Ltd.
Sussex, England

The Book Guild Ltd.
25 High Street,
Lewes, Sussex.

First published 1992
© Harry Dale 1992
Set in Baskerville
Typesetting by APS,
Salisbury, Wiltshire.
Printed in Great Britain by
Antony Rowe Ltd.,
Chippenham, Wiltshire.

A catalogue record for this book is
available from the British Library

ISBN 0 86332 800 8

FOREWORD

Perseverance, a caustic wit and determination to achieve a place in Britain's Air Force are at work in the heart of Arthur 'Dixie' Day, hero of this war story with a difference. The difference is that the story focuses on Day's flight training in the southern United States rather than on his actual war record.

The frustrations of unfamiliar customs and surroundings, of uninspired petty officialdom, and of constant harassment by his superiors wear almost unendurably on Dixie. He has only his courage, his biting humour and his far-off (perhaps too far-off) wife for comfort.

Day is the victim of anti-British prejudice and open hostility, even unwarranted efforts to sabotage his flying career. The problems arising from differences in dialect and temperament only strengthen the resolve of this maverick. Earning the chance to fly for England is far more important, so on the brink of losing this chance, he risks everything in one bold stroke. The friction between trainer and student finally triggers enmity into action with far-reaching and unexpected consequences.

This novel is rich in reflections of the attitudes and customs of the time. The descriptions of flight training and exercises ring true, which is not surprising considering that the author himself served in Bomber Command in Europe with twenty-two operations to his credit. The slang, the nicknames, the servicemen's ditties, all contribute to the flavour, and combine to give the reader the sense of being right there, a part of all the practical jokes, the rigorous training, and as a witness to the unexpected.

E. Hubbard

1

'Why do you want to fly?' The Wing Commander glared at me with probing eyes. I guess with three comfortable tapes around your cuff, probing eyes go with the territory.

It must have been me who answered; I was the only other one there.

'I feel the only way we are going to beat the enemy, sir, is to out-fly them.'

'Yes, but why you? You are already twenty-five years old. Shouldn't you be leaving flying to a younger man?'

'But sir, should I be leaving to a youngster something that I could probably do better myself?'

He glanced at the document in front of him. 'I see you are married man with a child. Why you?'

'I have more to lose, sir, if we let this war slip through our fingers.'

His eyes softened somewhat. He scribbled something at the bottom of the page, and I knew I WAS IN . . . .

Soon I was on the train again, winging my way back to my 'parent station' in the Midlands, and what a contrast in the two journeyings. Those bunched-up feelings of inferiority had dispersed, leaving me confident and eager for the next phase.

When I had arrived at the Aircrew Selection Board at RAF Station Padgate, I'd found I was one of twenty other hopefuls, a dozen of whom were Dutch university students and a quiet, self-contained bunch of chaps. By degrees we prepared to 'turn in', as we had a demanding day ahead of us. Until then, I was pretty confident about the educational exam; I had prepared myself in the preceding months, and had boned up on my maths. I was ready for the test. But how about the medical? Everyone knew that was a stinker. Would my anxiety to pass send my blood pressure soaring?

As is usual in a barrack-room, there is a clown with a big voice who has to carry on a conversation with a similar mental case at the far end of the room. Eventually I protested.

'How about quietening down and letting us get some shut-eye?'

'Supposing I don't want to. Who's going to make me?'

A dozen Dutchmen threw aside their blankets and said: 'Vee vill . . . .'

'Oh well, all right then,' mumbled the clown.

Although my formal education was by no means extensive, I did well on the written test and soon found myself being hauled, shoved, and prodded by the M.O. He was about to take my blood pressure when the phone rang in the annexe, and he went to answer it. During the brief time that he was away, I reached over to the washbasin and poured myself a cold, refreshing, and I'm sure life-giving, drink. I was on a pretty even keel when the M.O. returned. No problem.

After several weeks of waiting, I was posted to an Initial Training Wing in Newquay, Cornwall. We were housed in a respectable seaside hotel and on rather meagre rations. We were harassed, drilled, and instructed, apparently to discover what our breaking point was. Long cross-country runs usually followed hours of 'square bashing'. I was always somewhat relieved to hear at least one pair of feet pounding along behind me.

During a Sunday's 'fire piquet' I found some sheets of styrofoam in the hotel basement. Immediately, I recognized an ally. This super-light, rigid material was easily cut and fashioned to fit the back-pack of our equipment. I could foresee at some point in time that we would be sent on a route march in full pack and equipment. I found a loose board (which I felt also contributed to my cause) in the floor of my bedroom.

Though the discipline was harsh, the officers and NCOs were a clean, healthy bunch with lots of reserve of lung power. Our instruction covered airmanship, signals, hygiene, pyrotechnics, ship recognition, aircraft recognition, navigation and a few other things. Navigation was the subject they stressed. It was obvious that they weren't going to allow an airman to be floating around in the sky and not knowing which portion of the sky he was in.

The air was bracing. The Atlantic breezes sent huge waves

lashing the shore. We learned to surf. In addition to the demands of the normal routine, my name appeared on the notice board for extra Morse instruction. This meant a two-mile walk each way to the signals hut on the top of a hill outside of town. How I hated Morse.

Gradually we were approaching the end of the twelve-week course. We hadn't had our route march yet, and the next day was to be the navigation exam. It was going to be a brute: three hours in a room where the clock went round at twice the normal speed. We soberly contemplated this and studied like beavers until 'lights out'. We then collapsed on to our beds for some well-earned shut-eye . . . and then: 'On parade!' 'Full pack and equipment!' 'Great-coats will be buttoned up to the neck!'

Of course I had done some useful preparation against such an unpleasant happening. I shuffled all my heavy equipment into the floor where the loose board was and slid my styrofoam liner into my back-pack. It was such a neat fit that the sergeant drew the attention of the squadron to it. Having assembled in the hotel parking lot, we moved out into the blackening night at a stout clip.

Mothers of your well-brought-up sons, would you recognize them as they stepped into the night, singing a well-loved marching song like *Stars of the Evening*?

> Stars of the evening, beautiful and bright,
>   Up your flipping pipe,
> Stars of the evening,
>   Shining on the shit-house door.
> Of all the things I'd like to be, I'd like to be a crab.
>   I'd like to be a crab.
> I'd like to climb up-on the COs balls and drive the
> bastard mad.
>   Yes, I'd drive the bastard mad.
> Of all the things I'd like to be, I'd like to be a ring
>   Upon a lady's hand,
> And everytime she changed her pants,
>   I'd view the promised land
> Yes, I'd view the promised land.

We had two ex-policemen in our mob, big guys with strides

of about four feet. Heaven help me if I had not evened out this physical disparity with a spot of home-made justice. I passed the Nav test comfortably in the middle of the pack.

I led the class in Morse, both on the buzzer and the Aldis lamp. McLusky, who had previously been employed as a wireless operator aboard a merchant ship, failed signals. The class, who had been aware that I was having trouble *getting* Morse, congratulated me and then went to commiserate with McLusky. Great fellows, these.

We were issued our flying gear now, and it was reassuring to know how much thought had been put into our comfort, safety, and well-being. Colin Campbell, a roommate of mine, had sent home for his golf gear, maintaining that his handicap was forty-eight. Now with three kit-bags to lug around, I would imagine his handicap was considerably in excess of that. Dennison, my other roommate, a lad with everything, who came from a good family and a public school education, made a serious error of lining up twice for rice pudding dessert, and was spotted by the cook. He naturally admitted it, was charged, and was found guilty of stealing. With that on his records, he would never be granted a commission. A rotten shame, that. He would have made an excellent officer.

It was then with mixed feelings that we boarded a train for leave and whatever the powers-that-be had in store for us. Meanwhile, leave had letter-writing beat all to hell.

Next we found ourselves lodged in the service flats in St John's Wood, London.

By now the RAF had a certain investment in its cadets, and restraint and confinement became a practised art. Various holding units were set up. Flying training (involving night flying) could only take place under the malevolent eyes of our intruding enemy, so the further training of cadets slowed.

We found ourselves for a while living under canvas in Ludlow, Shropshire. In a high-walled, enclosed estate at Heaton Park near Manchester – anywhere to keep us available, disciplined, and healthy.

Although St John's Wood was in the heart of London, most of that metropolis was out of bounds to us, or as the Yanks put it, 'off limits'. We were not allowed out of that restricted area until the stores closed. This presented a problem, especially to me, as my daughter was to have her first birthday quite soon.

11

'Buy her something that is cuddly and makes a noise,' wrote my wife (little knowing what she was asking). It had to be a 'midday', this illicit shopping foray; and choosing my first opportunity, I was striding it out purposefully, when a service police corporal fell into step with me.

'Where are you going, cadet?'

'Oh, er, Abbey Lodge, Corp.'

Abbey Lodge, adjacent to the Lord's Cricket Ground, had been converted to a general administrative and medical centre for cadets.

'Why?'

'I have a hell of a toothache, Corp. Perhaps they can give me something for it.'

'Maybe,' he said, and still plodded along at my side.

When we came to the dental office, he pushed his way in. 'This man has tooth troubles,' he asserted.

'Sit there and open your mouth wide,' said the dental officer, and at this point the corporal seemed to think of other places he'd rather be.

From there I set out at a trot for Oxford Street and found a black and white fluffy dog that squeaked.

The girl behind the counter firmly refused to wrap it for me. 'Haven't you heard there's a war on?' the little bitch enquired.

Getting back to the squadron, on parade, was practically impossible in the time available. Not easy to pass inspection, dribbling blood from the corners of my mouth and concealing a rather noticeable fluffy dog. But at the crucial moment, a practice air raid alert sounded.

In Ludlow we were required to build a road – not that a road needed building, but that kind of activity is easily supervised and is a perfect ploy for keeping young, healthy men out of mischief. They needed ambulance drivers, and they accepted my application. Most of my duties were 'stand-by', but on every third day I took a trip into Hereford with a patient.

The RAF had commandeered for its temporary sick quarters a modern residence, set in a couple of acres. What was more important to me was the fruit hanging from the branches of the small bushes – black and red currants, raspberries, and goose-berries. Within earshot of the phone, and with a good view of the approaches, I quietly harvested several big cartons of the fruit which I took to the station at Hereford while I was waiting for the patient to return. I was able to build up a happy liaison with a small jobber in Covent Garden. It was somewhat embarrassing for me when I rushed to the place where they had dragged a drowned cadet out of the river, and he had to share the ride with a few cartons of lush fruit.

Our order for entertainment came suddenly and rather unexpectedly and found me off-guard. Tommy Farr, one of my tent mates, asked: 'What's the trouble, Dixie?'

I told him I had a couple of boxes of fruit on my hands.

'I'll look after them for you, Dixie,' he promised.

'How the hell can you?' I asked. 'You're confined to camp like the rest of us.'

He winked and disappeared with the boxes. He later handed me ten shillings.

'How did you manage to get out of camp?' I asked.

'I didn't, Dixie, my boy. I sold them to the Officers' Mess.'

At last we were to make contact with aircraft. It was quite noticeable. The closer you got to flying, the more relaxed the atmosphere got, and the more imagination went into the cooking. I am not saying it was a better meal, but it was different.

And so to Grading School. At some time in the past we had been consulted as to what our preferences were regarding our vocation: pilot, navigator or bomber.

It was nice to be asked.

We knew that in what capacity we served would be decided for us inflexibly by the powers-that-be. Yet in a couple of weeks, devoted to ground instruction with twelve hours' dual flying tuition, we would know where we stood.

A certain easement of the rigorous discipline could now be noticed. Meals were served with just that touch of imagination we were not accustomed to. Getting out of the gate was a snap.

Sleeping quarters were small. I shared a hut with just one other cadet, a chap named Antell. At least that was the name inscribed big and bold on the side of the cabin trunk he dragged into the hut. There was no introduction. Until he was strapped into his cockpit on the day of his test flight, no word ever passed between us, though I heard him making it known in the Mess that he was ex-C.I.D., which, no doubt, explained to some extent our brief relationship. He was twice my size. He

13

was dour, and the grim look on his face never changed. Most chaps I can get along with quite comfortably. This individual I could not like. Firstly, he went to the local pub every night, something I could not afford. Around midnight he would come blundering into the hut; switch on the lights; tug off my blankets, throw a wet, smelly, gritty, muddy mongrel dog into my bed; and replace the blankets. This is good fun if it happens once, but he seemed to have the ability to entice a stray (a different one each night) to follow him.

Lights being turned on above my head when I'm sleeping can be a disagreeable disturbance, so I found a broom just long enough to reach the light switch from my bed. Darkness apparently did not appeal to Antell. I heard his heavy breathing as he groped for, and found, the broom. He smashed it over his knee and wordlessly retired to bed. Remonstrance wouldn't serve any purpose. He just didn't place any value on my friendship. For that he had to pay. I gave considerable thought as to how this must be done.

My wife had sent me a small parcel, and delightfully it contained a minute pot of homemade jam. I knew she had sacrificed some of her tightly rationed sugar to make it. I knew she hoped it would bring me some pleasure. With any luck at all, it was going to – and how!

I smeared a light film of the sticky substance around the cuffs and the neckbands of the clothes hanging in Antell's clothes cupboard during one of his jaunts to the village. I gave similar attention to his remaining attire in the morning when he went for his shower.

This was the day of our test ride. Some of our group had already soloed. I hadn't. The day was grey and chilly, and the line of Tiger Moths looked small, delicate, and remote at the far side of the airfield known as the 'flight'. Although we had been short of cigarettes for a few days, most of us managed to find something to crack a joke about. Not so Antell; he was looking distinctly peevish and ill-at-ease. As we would be taking our turns in alphabetical order, he would be first, myself second, for takeoffs. It was the duty of the cadets to strap their comrades into their cockpit. It was I who mounted the wing root to make sure Antell was secure, but not too comfortable. He kept passing an irritable finger around the back of his collar.

There was a mammoth crane attached to some construction work quite close to our circuit pattern. As the 'gipsy' motor roared into life, I shouted: 'You don't have to worry about the crane. It's well out of your path.'

And so they went bumping over the field to the takeoff point on the farther perimeter, my prayers going with them. It had not been a happy day for Antell, I'm afraid. I had heard him trying to bum cigarettes. None of us could oblige. We had high hopes, however, that the NAAFI (that is the Navy, Army and Air Force Institute) van, which regularly visited the flights with urns of tea and buns, might have a small ration of cigarettes aboard.

There was a roar from the distant perimeter, and soon Antell was steering a groggy path towards us and then staggered uneasily into the air and away. Ten minutes later he droned back into our ken. He seemed to be making a beeline for that crane. He seemed fascinated by it. Soon he descended and was helped to alight.

'Thumbs down!' said the instructor. 'Froze to the controls. Couldn't get him to relax.'

My turn now. I had a massive instructor. He literally overflowed the cockpit in front of me, and I was hard put to peer around his generous shoulders as we 'essed' toward our takeoff point. I went through the well-rehearsed cockpit drill, feeling happy. I am not normally a vindictive type, but seeing Antell strike out sort of gave me a glow.

'The cloud is quite thin,' shouted my instructor. 'We'll go up through it and do a few stalls and spins.'

Stalls and spins didn't bother me that day.

'OK. Back to the field and land!'

Well, I tried. I reduced height in the prescribed manner and, on the final approach, I seemed just the right height to stall her in. I waited and I waited and then the earth came up and hit me. There was a grunting and a twanging, such as is not heard from a well-behaved plane. I edged the stick forward and opened the throttle, climbed into the circuit, and came in for what I was sure was going to be a perfect 'pancake'. Lo and behold, the same thing took place. No instructor in the world would stand for a double botch, and yet curiously enough I was not dismayed. I flew a little deeper into the down-wind leg, and then I spotted the NAAFI-wagon approaching the flights.

My guardian angel took over. He banked me to port with just sufficient opposite rudder to keep us straight and then swung the stick in the other direction to spill off a bit of unnecessary air. He then held the stick right into my gut, and the little plane landed, softly as a butterfly on a summer bloom, within twenty yards of the wagon.

The straps restraining my instructor slapped loosely against the fuselage and before you could say 'knife' he was standing there with a mug of clouding tea and five cigarettes in his other hand.

'You'll make a first-rate pilot, Day,' he said.

My official designation was Leading Aircraftsman A. Day, U/T pilot. '*Any man who comes between him and his pilot wings does so at his peril.*'

Back to Heaton Park, Manchester, and a mansion set on a hill, amid an eighty-acre estate and surrounded by a ten-foot wall which was patrolled by service police. We were drilled and paraded with a mindlessness that was only just endurable – but we were selected pilots, and who was going to step out of line?

The only other activity was eating, and we lined up for grub practically as soon as the last meal was over. We lined up in pairs, and the forward progression was so slow that we would make chess sets out of thin sheet leather with slots cut to represent the squares and small 'men' of pieces of flat leather. These makeshift chessboards were hung by a tab from the nearly motionless collar of the chap in front of you.

Only one side of the estate was occupied. The wasteland north of the mansion (now used as the station HQ and Officers' Mess) was not put to any use and was not visible from the mansion.

I sauntered in that direction one evening after dark, and I thought I heard a faint trickling sound, the slight movement of water. Could it be a small stream was somewhere there in that wasteland? If it was in there, then there must be some means of it getting out. I was interested. I had a similar problem.

Next day I made a point of being noticed, so that if my presence was required, everyone knew I was around somewhere. Then I moved slowly over the rise and followed the small stream that I had discovered until it came to a wall. For its convenience, then, it exited through a four-foot diameter ceramic pipe. The depth of the water flowing through was about eight inches. I was somewhat elated with this find and did not begrudge the physical exertion entailed in carrying hefty rocks down the little gully to make stepping stones. Soon I had a private (yes, very private) entrance to Heaton Park.

I made frequent use of this sneak-away but was always alive to the possibility that a posting might come up, in which case it would be to my advantage to be around. Such a posting did crop up – we were sent down to South Wales on an engines course.

This was another holding ploy but a valuable and interesting one. We learned how to strip down a Rolls Royce engine, reassemble it, and make it run. this would be very valuable information indeed if any of us ever had a Rolls that wasn't performing properly.

Life became a tedious and complex business. The Air Force wanted us where they could lay their hands on us at short notice; and the speed of our further training was dependent, to a considerable degree, on the whim of the intruder forces from Germany. Some trainees were sent to Canada, others to Africa, while there was a rumour going around via the 'latrineograph' that the Americans were making training available to us.

These sombre speculations occupied my mind as the train once more took us to that hallowed precinct, Heaton Park. We now had two kit-bags to haul and find room for. Wacker Wright sat astride his in the corridor, murmuring *Little Miss Muffet*:

> Little Miss Muffet
>   She sat on her tuffet,
> Her knickers all tattered and torn.
>   It wasn't a spider
> That sat down beside her,
>   But Little Boy Blue with the horn.

I was keenly looking forward to our arrival at Heaton Park. The procedure that worked so well before would work again: get in everybody's hair, take an unhurried stroll over the hill, and follow that small stream to the pipe under the Oldham road to the outside world. But that evening, as I ambled along towards the crest of the hill, I became uneasily aware that I was not alone. Other cadets seemed to be moving in the same

17

direction; when I reached the crest and looked down, I saw at least a hundred cadets lining up to use my pipe. Clearly this was no place for me – I hated crowds.

Why not approach this thing through the proper channels? My stepping stones being used by the common herd, the uninitiated, had suddenly crystallized a thought, a line of thought to which I had been a stranger these many weeks: 'Try going through the proper channels.'

2

I, Arthur Day, wish to state with emphasis that it was not my
wish to take my flying training in the United States. For one
thing, Eve was joyously pregnant. We had a lovely little
copper-headed daughter, Penelope; Eve was going to give
Pennie a little brother – or bust. Eve wasn't the bustie type. Of
course we'd talked it over from all angles. Eve pointed out that
the government was particularly solicitous of small children
and pregnant women: orange juice, cod liver oil, that sort of
thing.

'Who knows how long the war will last? If we wait till then,
Pennie might be five.'

It was well on the cards that I should have to take some of
my training abroad, but it was by no means certain.

'If you're sent away,' my wife ventured tremulously, 'it will
be something to occupy me.'

There was, of course, that other consideration: there was a
big, heaven-sent, stirring war going on, and I was more than a
little concerned with its evolvement and outcome. In addition,
I had no particular liking for 'Uncle Sam'. All his ballyhoo, his
fabulous riches, his fast living and his wisecracks were fine at
the cinema as entertainment and escapism. It did seem difficult
to reconcile this scenario with the hard and often humdrum
facts of wartime living. I had bad vibrations about it.

At the inevitable interview with the 'brass':

'Permission to speak, sir?'

'Speak.'

'Request to be allowed to continue my training in this
country, sir.'

'Why?'

'We are training Czechs, Poles and Hindustanis in this
country, sir. These men have very little preference where they

19

train, and I have certain domestic obligations.'

'I'm going to grant you two weeks leave in order for you to attend to your "domestic obligations". By then, your sailing orders should be through. Request refused.'

The sailing was enacted by the brand-new liner, *Queen Elizabeth*, on her maiden voyage.

To meet this majestic lady of the seas, we had, of course, been jammed like cattle into a blacked-out train. No heat, practically no light, absolutely no information regarding our destination – par for the course, I guess. What besotted prune thinks up these playful little picnics? 'We have enough men to fill fourteen carriages; let's cram 'em all into four.'

Towards the dawn, we were tossed about from track to track with about as much finesse as a terrier shows to a rabbit. This indicated that we were approaching a built-up area of some kind. We started to unlock shoulders and tried to stretch. At about this juncture we were thrown quite heavily against the compartment wall, as the clown who was driving this train jammed on his brakes. The stunned oaf had all night to slow down in, but no, he had to bring our journey to a close with a flourish. Blast him!

The sign said 'Greenock.'

'Och aye, Greenock.' All the young airmen knew Greenock; even those hailing from the farthest tip of Cornwall knew Greenock, knew it well, and started 'och ayeing' in what they considered a genuine Highland burr.

Meanwhile we were struggling into 'webbing', namely (a) two large backpacks, (b) one side satchel or 'small kit', and (c) followed by a water drinking bottle or 'canteen', a saucepan with folding-down handle, and a respirator, all girded around with belts, straps, and buckles in order to make movement practically impossible, and breathing doubtful. Thus garbed, we struggled out on to a foggy platform to the guard's van, where we retrieved our two sausage-shaped kit-bags, which we swung panier-fashion around our necks. A pinnace awaited us at the end of the docks. I always thought that a pinnace was propelled by oars. This one had a smoke stack, so presumably it had an engine.

'Step up smartly, now. Move further forward.' Standing-room only again, damn 'em.

Small breaks in the fog showed us the docks we were just

leaving, with their cranes and derricks coated with a mixture of frost and moisture, grey, motionless and forbidding. As we cast off and got underway, a young, piping voice broke into a chorus: 'Sailing Down the Clyde' or 'Up the Clyde' – I just don't remember. The singer's mother would, no doubt, have loved that voice. I didn't think much of it.

As we surged smoothly but relentlessly forward, the plaintive voice of foghorns called to us, and the remote and mournful ships' hooters lamented our passing. Even the gulls were complaining. After what seemed a half hour, the engine room telegraph clanged and the motor stopped. The pinnace seemed motionless, but the deck-hands made their way unhurriedly forward. Then gradually we were confronted by it: a wall of steel, grey-painted, massive, unyielding. No-one could see the extent of its towering sides; the deck rail and the name were obscured by fog, but everyone recognized her immediately.

'It's the *Elizabeth*.'

'Oh, sure.'

They not only knew her tonnage displacement but her power, capacity, the works. Everyone was so completely versed in information on this new liner (what with wartime security's lack of gossip) that they must have lived the last four years in the shadow of its slipway. Where the heck was I?

The oil-slick sea made sporadic passes up the liner's side with as much effect as a rhinoceros being chastised with a sprig of maidenhair fern. Nothing else moved. Then somewhere up above a bell rang, and immediately a huge section of the steel plate, which formed a part of the ship's belly hinged at the bottom just above the Plimsoll line, fell away. It was rather like the drawbridge of some moated castle. We scrambled up this platform into the dimly lit bowels of the ship to the cries of 'Up the Queen,' 'Good old Liz,' and 'Who the heck ordered this rowing boat?' Well, when you're eighteen going on nineteen, or nineteen going on twenty, how else do you embark? I was twenty-eight going on twenty-nine, and to me the whole thing seemed to bear a bizarre resemblance to an appendectomy – only in reverse.

Twenty-four bodies were allocated to a cabin. The souls, if any, were supercargo. The cabin was rather as I had pictured an opium smoker's den: bunks from deck to ceiling. My bunk was third up. I had just festooned the end of it with my small

21

kit and harness and was busily lying on my bunk and inspecting the one above me when Larry Kratz ambled in from an adjacent cabin and squatted on the bunk opposite mine.

'How've you been, Dixie?' he asked.

'Bloody horrible, thanks.' Out of the corner of my eye I looked him over. Fresh, young, clear-eyed, with just the suggestion of lines which would later indicate earnest honesty beginning to form above his nose. Right at present they betokened innocent naivety. 'Where did I see you last?'

'Hut 23, Heaton Park. Remember?'

'Afraid not, young Kratters. The only thing I remember about that benighted establishment is that it was raw cold: pitilessly, remorselessly, rotten cold.'

'Sure, Dixie. It's all entered in my diary. All through the winter they issued us with green twigs and coke for firing. I remember the first night you arrived there. We were trying to light the stove with that unlikely fuel. You took one look, moseyed off into the blackout, and came back around dawn with a sizable roll of tar-paper under your arm.'

'Is that right?'

'You know damn well it's right. When I woke up that morning, I saw you heaving up the floor lino and stashing the combustible loot underneath. Where did you swipe it?'

'I guess it don't matter now, kid. That was perhaps one of the best-kept secrets of the war. Nobody knew about me. That roll of tar-paper I rived from the roof of the Service Police piquet hut.'

'And weren't there any SPs about?'

'Naturally. There was one in there all the time and others booking in and out and making entries and so forth all night.'

'You mean you were up on that roof riving that covering from their shack and they didn't hear you, and they only about four feet below you?'

'Slowed me down a lot, kid, but I suppose it was just something I had to do. I remember it was bone-grasping cold and dark as the inside of an elephant. But you do what you have to do.'

He sat there for a while. I had the impression that he was remembering that glowing stove at Hut 23 at the RAF Station Holding Unit, Heaton Park. Heaton Park had a wall all around it, ten feet high, patrolled on the outside by sentries. I

22

believe it was brought into existence by some industrial magnate who did not enjoy the look of his fellow man and certainly had no intention of being seen by him. All in all, Heaton Park was the ideal place to hold the many thousands of air crew cadets who were awaiting shipment overseas to train. Row after row of Nissen huts had been erected to house 'the very cream of this nation's manhood' (Winston's description, not mine). A Nissen hut is a corrugated iron structure. The corrugations were especially suited to radiating any heat outwards. There was a fire bucket, invariably frozen solid and painted a vivid red, beside each bed. This was typical of the blunderheaded British approach to war. An edict would be passed that all homes having iron railings must have them cut down and hauled to the iron foundry where they would be converted into red-painted fire buckets. The thought of those metal 'igloos' going up in smoke no doubt constituted a massive threat. Happy days.

'We've sailed, you know, Dixie,' Larry observed.

'Oh, really? No streamers? No bands playing? Pretty poor show, what?'

'I take it, Dixie, there are a few tiny items about the war effort and this branch of the forces that don't exactly appeal to you. Have you always been a rebel?'

'I don't think I consider myself a rebel, young Kratters, but to a limited degree I like to look on myself as a freethinker. All our training so far has had one primary purpose: namely to obey instantly, instinctively, uncomplainingly; to carry out death, destruction, and devastation whenever and wherever some remote person desires that we should. Right? Now that should pretty well close the deal, shouldn't it? Ah, but no. While we are waiting to acquire this skill at creating mayhem, our lives are to be rendered as unpleasant as possible.'

'But don't you think the same thing is happening to the young aspirants on the other side? The vaunted Luftwaffe types must have their training and conditioning handed out to them in a very similar way.'

'I would assume so, young Kratters. Let's say it does, right? Then everything is in perfect balance. He's fighting for his Fatherland under rather unattractive conditions; and we are going in to bat for our Motherland with, shall we say, a similar scenario.'

'What are you getting at, Dix?'

'Merely if that was the bone and complete essence of the matter, it would be much more humane, progressive, and sensible to call a halt – declare it a draw.'

'And?'

'Well, that would leave a void, an unresolved factor. The Germans, the Nazis, or whatever you like to call them, have incurred our righteous and wrathful indignation. Does this sound preachy? Let it. Those sewer rats have got to be returned to the sewer before the world can get on and live. To answer your question concerning my tendency to rebel, this is my war. Authority (be it officer or NCO): Obstruct me at your peril.'

'I think the point you're making is that you'll suffer fools but not gladly. You'll go along with this bull discipline, because to stay on the course you've got sweet damn-all choice.'

'Is that so?'

'And, as your friend and well-wisher, Dixie, old horse, don't do anything to antagonize the bastards. Save it for Jerry. I should hate to hear you'd led with your chin and finished up doing a stretch in the glasshouse. Do they have such a thing over there, I wonder?'

'Assuming you mean Canada, and assuming that's where we are bound, it's pretty certain they have some kind of glasshouse, pokey, or jug. I believe the Yanks call theirs a "stockade".'

'I'm taking bets that we're for the States.'

'You seem pretty sure of yourself, young Kratters. Has this news just leaked through on the latrineograph?'

'No, my sister told me.'

'Come again?'

'My sister in New York. She helps at the stage-door Canteen, doling out coffee and doughnuts to Allied servicemen on leave there.'

'You arouse my interest, young Kratters. How does she spend the rest of her time?'

'She's a doctor at the New York General. It's during her stint behind the coffee bar that she hears quite a lot about the training schedules and things. She says the Americans have ten airfields in regular use for the training of British pilots. Some of them have a graduating class about now, and I'm betting we're

24

going to one of those places as freshman replacements. Do you want to make a friendly wager?'

'Thanks, no. But you arouse my curiosity. How does your sister in the face of all this tight security, get this information across the pond?'

'Oh hell, Dixie, you can still send air letters across. They may be censored, of course, but if she's got anything interesting to say, she writes it in Yiddish.'

'And do you understand that lingo?'

'Just like you understand English, Dixie old horse.'

'So, young Kratters. You are a Jew? I didn't know.'

'Why the hell should you? You don't get in the middle of the parade square and yell, "I'm British of Anglo-Saxon extraction," so why the hell should I? Although I'm of British strain, we are a proud race; we keep our pride tucked out of sight; we are aware of our vulnerability, but distinctly aware, old horse, of our strength, our ability to endure.'

'Well, well, well,' I said, somewhat embarrassed and nonplussed. 'I joined up to save the Jews, and I believe this is the first time I've ever met one close up.'

'You've sure led a sheltered existence, Dixie old horse.'

At this point Cadet Farley strode through the door with his towel around his shoulders and shaving gear in his hand. 'Get off my bunk, you little whoremaster,' he said.

'You do me far to much credit,' grinned Larry. 'I was never more than a whoremaster's apprentice.'

'Come on, young Kratters,' I said. 'Let's go and eat. I suppose you've located the cookhouse by now?'

'Aboard ship they don't call them cookhouses, Dixie. We will wend our way to the dining saloon. They serve up the grub at a cracking pace and give you real white bread.'

'Well, I'll be darned. I wonder what mental pygmy thought that one up – grey brown wartime bread suited me a treat.'

After the meal, which was adequate and well-cooked, we went our separate ways to write letters; and so began our shipboard routine. Each cabin had a cabin orderly, and he had a roster pinned to the back of the door. You left your bunk and shaved and performed your ablutions according to your position on the list. The floor space only allowed four to leave their bunks together. After meals came lifeboat drill. Sometimes you would stand in the dumb line-up for a chilly hour, while the grey Atlantic threw playful little helpings of itself in your face. Sometimes (the fortunate times), before you had located your lifeboat station, the drill was over and you were swept below by the concentration of bodies leaving the boat deck.

Once clear of the home waters, the mighty vessel ignored the March winds and heavy, thudding waves and forced her way relentlessly into that limitless expanse of water, water, and further water – alone, unheralded, and unescorted. Completely oblivious to any untoward element, each time she buried her bows afresh into those sullen, grey swells, her massive propellers cleared of restraint, she transmitted a shuddering fury of vibration throughout her entire length. The thousands of drab-clad servicemen that swarmed her many decks and holds with studied nonchalance quickly adapted to and then ignored their unaccustomed environment.

Unaffected by any motion sickness, I found a spot just inside the forward porthole where I could scan the oncoming ocean – just in case anything of interest came into view. Nothing did. On the second day out, three or four sergeants set up tables beneath where I sat and set up a tombola, or housie-housie game (later to be called bingo). Larry Kratz stood at my elbow, watching the other ranks being exhorted to try their luck at the really big winnings.

'Do you think those NCOs who are running the game are Jewish?' he asked me.

I glanced at them. 'No, I wouldn't think so, young Kratters. Why?'

'It just occurred to me that when the poor slobs who are so eager to win, find that all their pay is gone, do you know what they're going to say? "I was Jewed".'

I lolled there with the big butterfly nut that secured the porthole, in close, persuasive contact with my mischievous elbow.

'Make for the door,' I grunted.

He gave a start. 'For cripes sake, Dixie, don't try anything.' He then shrugged and sidled to the door. I had just joined him when the porthole blew in, and a shrieking wet wind stormed in and sent the cards and other items of the game, soggy and forlorn, into the scuppers. We could still hear the cries of rage and threats as we mingled with the crowd in the nearest companionway.

When we reached the cabin, Farley was sitting on his bunk with a glossy magazine on his lap. 'Ah! friend Cats. How's things in the jolly old alley today?'

'Your attempt at sociability is very touching, Farley. Just remember the "r", will you. The name is Kratz.'

Farley, however, was not through with his provocation and proceeded to trot out the old barrack-room ditty:

Cats on the roof-top,
　Cats on the tiles,
Cats with the syphilis,
　Cats with the piles,
Cats with their arse-holes wreathed in smiles,
　As they revelled in the joys of fornication.

Larry Kratz seized the magazine and made a jocular attempt to stifle the noise with it. Farley got annoyed and, hopping from his bunk, took a swing at Kratz. Fortunately for him, the liner gave a lurch, and a fist whistled past his ear. In the scuffle that ensued, Larry Kratz was giving away about eight inches in height and about forty pounds in weight; but after a half a minute had gone by, Farley was a squirming heap on the floor. Larry strode over to the door and closed it quietly behind him. To show that I didn't attach any importance to the affray, I got out my writing-pad for a letter to home.

My sweet little Eve,

　We are pushing our way, in a business-like manner, across the Atlantic. What a waste and a shame that you aren't here beside me. One day we will take a trip like this together . . . .

On the third day out, the lowering grey skies disclosed an aircraft flying at about 500 feet, and to our considerable relief we identified it as a Sunderland flying-boat. It made a tight circuit around us, and then a door in its midships slid open and we saw an airman sitting there with an Aldis lamp resting on his crossed legs. Soon the lamp started to flash a familiar cadence. I reached for my fountain pen and an old envelope. 'Can you get any of it?' I asked Kratz, nearby.

'No, it's in code. Wonder what they're clacking about? Ah, now they're switching to plain language. Are you ready? G-O-O-D-B-Y-E A-N-D B-O-L-L-O-X. My goodness, that's pretty plain, isn't it. There's something quite fascinating about our jolly old language. Wouldn't you agree, old horse?'

On the fourth day, we awoke to find ourselves hard and fast in Halifax harbour. An old crow flew floppily over our funnels and lurched aimlessly off into some alternative airspace. Do they have crows in Canada? We were sort of expecting something rather more exotic. We surveyed what could be seen of Halifax across the harbour: little rows of detached matchbox-like houses, each with a totally different colour of roof. Well, I thought, we shall probably have the rest of the day to take in the scene – or better still to stretch out on the bunk and catch up with some sleep. On the way across we had been tossed out of our beds so often by the great ship's aquabatics, there hadn't been much sleep. When I reached the cabin, however, everyone was struggling into their equipment.

'Didn't you hear the Tannoy? We're the first lot to disembark.'

And so we were. Ten minutes later, we were shepherded into a high-pitched, warm, comfortable railway train. Six of us to a compartment: bags of room to stretch out and be human. What's wrong with these people? Didn't they realize there was a war on? The RTO was a greying, easy-going, fatherly type who seemed genuinely concerned whether we were hungry or not. Five minutes later we seemed to be moving, slowly and smoothly; I had the impression that someone had neglected to secure the handbrake, and we were slowly coasting downhill. Worldly-wise, I knew that very soon the mistake would be discovered, brakes would be jammed on, whistles would be frantically blowing, and we would probably be shunted on to some drab spur line to while the rest of the day away in solitary motionlessness. But no! We smoothly increased our speed until we were soon serenely curving our way through the outskirts of the city at a steady twenty knots.

It was still the tail-end of March; the territory we passed through was snow-covered, sad and uninviting. Practically all the land was wild, uncultivated bush. Dead trees sprawled around at random angles, awaiting silently the next stage of decay and decrepitude. We looked in vain for signs of wildlife:

for bears, moose, deer, or even rabbits. Nothing. We were soon sitting down to a well-cooked meal followed by ice cream. Ice cream? Ye gods!

At Truro, the train obligingly waited on the line while we dismounted, went into the town, and sat comfortably (under the benign and approving eye of the Chinaman who ran the café) and had coffee and doughnuts. At the expiry of half an hour, the train gave its educated 'All aboard' call and we resumed our journey to Moncton, New Brunswick.

3

Moncton, at the end of March. Let others, if they will, praise it or attempt to do it justice. I recollect that it was brown, chilly, and soggy. Not having overboots, I quickly abandoned any attempt to take a deeper than cursory look at the place. I squished back to the RCAF depot where my confederates were piling into taxis to go to get Chinese food.

'Coming, Dix?'

'No.' I had thinking to do.

The rumour that our 'batch' were bound for Jackson City, Oklahoma, was confirmed by a notice just inside the entrance. Kratz was completely happy.

'We've made it, Dix.'

'What the hell have we made?'

'America! You dim, decrepit old bastard. The USA! The land of promise! Just think, by sheer chance I shall be in the same country as my sister.'

'Bully for you, and congratulations to your sister.' I made the excuse that I had a letter to write. I didn't get around to writing it.

Through the mess hall, I picked my way to a rough stage at the further end, where I discovered a piano and bench. With my elbows on the closed lid, I began to ruminate. Who the hell needed America? The nasal twang? The wisecrack? The lumbering way of walking? I had crossed the pond with one thought in mind – to get my training done and to get back to the war and Eve. These Yanks were a race apart: different codes, different standards, different reasons for doing what they did. It meant that I would be travelling thousands of useless miles away from significant, purposeful living. I raised the piano lid and began to play quietly a part of Schubert's *Impromptu*.

'What you up to, Dix?' A half dozen of our crowd had climbed up on to the stage. 'Let's jazz it up there. How about giving us a bit of the right stuff? How about *Mobile*?'

'Don't know it.'

'Oh, balls! Of course you do. It's like *Coming Round the Mountain* with better words.' Soon they were belting it out, with me vamping.

> Oh! the CO is a bugger in Mobile.
>> Oh! the CO is a bugger in Mobile.
> Oh! the CO is a bugger and the Adjutant's another
>> And they bugger one another in Mobile.
> There's no paper in the bogs in Mobile.
>> There's no paper in the bogs in Mobile.
> There's no paper in the bogs, so we wait until it clogs,
>> Then we saw it off in logs in Mobile.
> There's a shortage of old whores in Mobile.
>> There's a shortage of old whores in Mobile.
> There's a shortage of old whores, but there's key holes in the doors
>> And there's knot-holes in the floors in Mobile.

This was followed by a dirge, which they rendered with solemn gusto, called *There Was an Old Monk of High Renown*. Most of the cadets, thronging around the piano with beer in hand, were re-mustered airmen, not volunteers like the bulk of our trainload. Whatever the peace-time Air Force found called upon to perform certainly seemed to have left them time to compose a volume of ribald ditties. I moved off the bench in order for Wacker Wright to do his solo turn:

> Please don't burn our shit-house down.
>> Mother has promised to pay.
> Father's away on the ocean,
>> Sister's in the family way,
> Brother dear has gonorrhoea
>> Times are very hard.
> So please don't burn our shit-house down,
>> Or we'll have to shit in the yard.

I stumbled off to my allotted barrack room, made my bed,

and crawled into it. But there was no sleep to be had that night. My immature confederates, excited, could not seem to have a thought in their heads without having it spill out through slack, childish lips. Blast them, never troubling to lower their voices.

I found it difficult to analyse my uneasiness about my potential sojourn in the States. It wasn't fear. Fear I could handle. Neither was it antipathy. More like revulsion. I could remember as a boy of five, we had a big rooster for Christmas dinner, and my older brother discovered the chopped-off leg could be manipulated by pulling the tendons. The scrawny, scaly foot could be made to distend its claws into a fierce and threatening attitude. My brother had a most hilarious day, chasing me with it. I was not frightened of it, just repelled by it.

I was happy to see the dawn greying the windows of the barrack room, and soon we were enjoying a savoury breakfast with piping hot, sweet coffee. Next we were issued our American uniforms: shirts and pants in a kind of pinker shade of khaki, together with good quality low, brown shoes to replace our boots. While the day was still young, we were entrained for Montreal.

Montreal was bright and bracing. It had stature; it had character; and wasn't it a bright idea for someone to put a mountain just where they needed one. The clear, blue sky and the brilliant sun assured us that God was in his heaven, and all was right with the world. In the three-hour stopover, we breasted the Royal Mountain, invigorated and exuberant – truly a Sunday morning to remember. On our way down the mountain, the sun flicked out long blue shadows on the snow. Our ears, however, had very little protection. Kratz and I were striding it out; Farley and Campbell were not far behind. Larry's ears were too much of a temptation for Farley, who paused to gather a fair-sized snowball. The shadows betrayed the approaching missile. We ducked. Not so the angular spinster who had just rounded the bend. The snowball caught her just north of the prayer book, which she clutched to her bosom.

'*Zut! Zut!*' she croaked, bending forward to shake out the snow. '*Ça alors c'est trop fort.*' The guilty Farley stepped forward to assist. He was rebuffed: '*Allez vous en maintenant.*'

'*Je vous demande pardon, Madame,*' groaned Farley in his

33

atrocious French.

'*Laissez moi passer,*' she commanded, threatening him with her prayer book.

A gendarme, who appeared from nowhere, gazed meaningfully after her retreating figure and at Farley. The gendarme was dead-pan but purposefully curious. What was Farley doing with his hand down the front of the lady's dress? Larry, whose French was reasonably good, tried to act as interpreter. No, Farley was not attacking the madam. They had never met before. They were just having fun. He and his friends were on their way to the railway depot to catch a train to Chicago. We edged our way slowly toward the city. The gendarme looked after us thoughtfully.

Chicago, on the edge of a still frozen lake, had very little snow left. It was gusty and dusty , noisy and utilitarian, beautifully set yet not attempting to capture admiring glances. Soiled newspapers and other garbage swirled around its unpainted corners. The 'Elevated' clanged and roared its way between the towering buildings. Our first taste of American cities was of short duration. Within the hour we had boarded a streamline express bound for Kansas City. As Farley joined the crowd of his waiting companions outside Dearborn Station, a wag at the rear had Farley's number: 'Farley fingered females, as fearless fliers do . . . .' Farley shrugged it off, or appeared to. Soon the train was leaving the 'canned meat capital of the world' behind. Twilight came, giving place to darkness; the great train was shrieking its way through the blackened void like a voracious, uncaring monster.

We reached Kansas City around ten at night. It was warm there – no need for a topcoat. With two hours' stopover, we set out to sample the delights of a mid-western city. The incredible wide Main Street was lined by stores and commercial properties of every description, each one modestly admitting to a superiority of some kind. The placards and billboards (almost overlapping one another) attested to it: 'The longest hot dog,' 'The slickest oil change,' 'The coolest beer . . . .' With but two hours to 'do' the city, we made no move to test these claims. Back to the train depot and the last leg of our trip. Jackson City, and the most colourful chapter in our lives, awaited us, somewhere up ahead. Excited anticipation triggered us. Only the most stolid stoics among us attempted to sleep. Across the great central plain of America, we sat in pairs chatting, yearning and yawning. Kratz and I hashed over general topics. And then . . . .

'What is it about Jews that you dislike?' he wanted to know.

'I've told you, young Kratters, my experience with Jews has been nonexistent. I haven't sought them out, and they apparently have not been aware of me. But I see you want to know what my impressions are, as confused, biased, and totally inaccurate as they may be. Right? Well now, first of all, how many do you find in the forces?'

'Oh, so that's the crap that's going around, eh? Most Jews have protected Jobs? Forget it, Dixie. It's a myth. Some highly intelligent Jews are holding positions that require their type of mentality; the government fastens them in. Take my family. My brother Si was washed overboard and drowned at the evacuation of Dunkirk. Benny, my second brother, is still in military hospital with extensive burns, sustained while defending Detling in 1940. Oh, when you prick us, we bleed. That only leaves my sister Miriam, and she's shifting heaven and earth to get back over there. We're in this bloody war up to our necks, as we should be. What else?'

'OK, OK, you young Israelite! You started this. Let's talk about women or something.'

'No. Carry on, old horse. You're doing just fine.'

'Well now, let's see. Somehow the Jews always seem to follow dubious ways of making a living. Money-lending, pawnbroking, the rag trade, show business, the dingy little corner store.'

'Stop there, Dixie. Do you realize how many trades were closed to us? Only in the last two decades have the professions been open to us. None of the good clubs will have us. Not until the turn of the century were we allowed to own land.' The rattle of the train over a bridge made him pause. 'Oh, Shylocks and Fagins there have been, possibly still are, but don't you realize that they are the natural outcome of discrimination and suppression?'

'No, I was not aware of that. Now what else? The Jews are clannish. They tend only to deal with other Jews.'

'Forget it, Dixie. My mother gets her ration books and my dad's pay and buys what we need where the money goes farthest. Apart from that, can you blame her if she goes where her needs are best understood?'

'You know, young Kratters,' I said, looking into his earnest young face, 'I'd very much like to meet your family some day.'

Larry didn't answer; he was asleep.

I went for a shave. The washroom would be in great demand a few hours from now. Dawn was presaged by airmen fumbling for a cigarette and the diminutive rasp of cigarette-lighters. Soon we were stretching, yawning and tousling our hair. The grey shadows of pre-dawn gradually took on colour, showing the rural scene that could have had a duplicate in almost any country. A farmhouse was set among sheltering trees, and in the adjoining farmyard two haughty geese, heads held high and unrelenting, interrogated a new-born calf. Lots of space here: the ruddy brown soil, lightly peppered with vegetation.

Larry tucked his shaving kit under his arm and headed for the washroom.

'If you're gonna shave, you'd better make it snappy. We should be there pretty soon,' I called after him.

Soon thereafter, the train began to lose speed. Someone was dragging on the reins, and the great beast was shrieking out its protest. We were reaching our gear and suitcases down from the luggage racks as Jackson City hove in sight. The great train rapidly adapted itself to the peaceful milieu; gone now was the shrieking, snarling monster, the leaper-over of chasms and things. Here was a mild-mannered dowager, sedately entering town, and no-one showed the least surprise to see us and her there. Hauling and grunting, we wrestled our stuff to the ground and wandered up and down outside the depot, looking for our transport. We spotted a yellow bus, marked Jackson City Airfield, and lurched in that direction. The train now, having rid itself of us, was starting to clang its bell and shriek its impatience to be off. Where was Kratz?

I rushed back and reboarded just as the conductor was slamming the door closed. The second washroom I came to had a two-foot splinter of wood (presumably from a nearby packing crate) wedged in the handle of the door. As I tugged this out, Kratz burst out like a pent-up cork from a bottle.

'Out of my way, you playful bastard,' he gasped, and sped down the carriage to where his goods and chattels were still sprawled. He brushed my help aside. 'Mischievous buggers like you should be in a zoo,' he asserted as we dismounted by means of the observation platform at the rear. By this time, we were a mile out of town.

'You don't think I had anything to do with that trick, do
you?'

'Oh no? Oh no? Who is it that's always up to some prank or
other and goes around looking innocent? No, don't bother to
help. Just keep your distance. Who else knew it was me in that
washroom? Eh?'

'Kratters, if you're crazy enough to believe guck like that, go
ahead.' And so we made our way back into town, Kratz loaded
down and sweating, me totally unencumbered. Both of us were
silent and indignant: very, very annoyed.

We had to ring the airfield for transport. They sent a bus.

The trip out to the airfield was an uncomfortable one, young
Kratz sitting there tight-lipped and aloof, probably wondering
what he had done that fate had landed him in the close orbit of
an uncontrollable practical joker. I was strengthening my
resolve that until my training was completed, it should get my
undivided attention; and I would not let any person or
inanimate object get in my way. The driver of the bus engaged
us in a one-sided conversation with a mesmerizing cadence,
mostly about the doings of his relatives, whom he seemed to
consider we knew quite well. After a while, we saw a couple of
hangars and a wind-sock on the skyline and were soon turning
through a gate marked Star School of Aeronautics. Wide
concrete paths led to low-pitched lecture rooms and dormitor-
ies. We were told that the adjutant wanted to see us. We
tapped on his door and walked in.

The adjutant, a Flight Lieutenant A.E. Mills, was a soft-
spoken uncle type, who obviously preferred the look of his desk
blotter, to us. 'This establishment,' he mentioned, 'Number 16
British Flying Training School has only three permanent RAF
personnel: the commanding officer, myself and the general
duties corporal. Until today, there has never been a need for
enforcing discipline. The trainees graduate from here as either
officers or NCOs with the exception of those who, for one
reason or another, fail to take advantage of the opportunities
here. Those we return to the Manning Depot, Toronto. There,
they are re-mustered to the ground staff and serve in that
capacity, in Canada, for the duration of hostilities. You may
not regard this as a warning, but I would be remiss if I didn't
attach a memorandum to your documents to the effect that

37

you were absent without leave, even before you arrived here. Dismissed.'

Larry and I dumped our gear in our assigned barrack room and went to the cafeteria, silently furious with each other.

In the afternoon we all assembled in the crew room adjoining a hangar and were given a lecture outlining what our course and training was to be. The chief instructor, an American civilian, gave this with a crooked cigar clamped to his back teeth. We would parade each morning at eight o'clock, after we had burnished our bed space, laid out our kit for inspection and had our breakfast. We then would be marched either to our lecture or to the crew room for flying. At noon we would be marched to the cafeteria for lunch and then marched to the post office to collect our mail, after which we would be marched to the crew room for lectures for the balance of the day.

This cigar-loving Yank, who said his name was Wilbur Nye, laid a great many things on the line. We would carry out the orders and assignments of our instructors and say 'Yes, sir' at all times. In the air, if the instructor said 'You've got her,' you would at all times reply 'I've got her, sir.' When flying solo, you would carry out and only carry out; the exercises assigned by the instructor. Anyone caught rat-chasing would be kicked off the course. 'Right now,' he droned on, 'I would like for to introduce you to our dispatcher. Here she is, Miss Betty Gowski. You will at all times carry out her orders without question.'

The first thing I noticed about our dispatcher was the shallowness of her brow. It was about as deep as a two-penny ice-cream sandwich. Below it roved a pair of black, malevolent eyes – calculating, insolent eyes. Apart from that, she was stocky and blousy. The plaquet of her skirt was obviously under considerable pressure. She chewed gum indolently.

I had long prided myself on being a judge of character. This female, on a scale of one to ten, wouldn't clear the starting line. A sense of rebellious outrage engulfed me. It was bad enough to be totally dominated by American civilians, but to be completely subordinate to some gutter-bred female was a gut blow I hadn't anticipated. The American students beamed at her toothfully: 'Hi, Beddy!' I pretended something else had caught my attention.

38

I waited impatiently for a glimpse of my instructor. There were about a dozen of them at the far end of the instructors' barrier. Some of them looked the part. Some were arguing and craggy while others were mild and colourless. The one I was assigned to was the only one with fur-lined goggles: a man of around twenty-four, of more than average height and build. The name tag on his patch pocket proclaimed him to be Meryl Vinter. He had a typically American face. Does that sound foolish? He had the typical slit eyes and slack mouth, and if you'd divided his face down the centre both halves would have matched perfectly. The owner of that face had never known want, had never known fear, had never known compassion. Four of us huddled around him and got the word.

'The aircraft you will be flying for the next two months will be the Steerman. After that you'll go to AT6s. The Steerman has a continental radial engine; it cruises at around 160 knots. To overcome the resistance to torque, its rudder is slightly offset to port, so you'll have to give opposite rudder as you gain speed for takeoff. Any questions? You will observed the flight pattern over the airfield at all times. You will takeoff into wind. At 500 feet you'll make a ninety to port, using a grade one climbing turn. Level out at a thousand. Make another ninety to port, and that puts you on the down-wind leg. OK so far? We leave the circuit by turning sixty degrees to starboard halfway down the down-wind leg. That angle again is sixty degrees. Not sixty-five. Not fifty-five. OK?'

All this was good, basic stuff. I wondered why we had to have it in a sort of huddle. Why not have it mimeographed and then we could sign a copy? How stupid of me – this was the instructors' chance to strut their stuff: 'See what a firm and resolute disciplinarian I am.'

'Any questions?' He seemed to be looking in my direction.

'Not that I can think of at the moment . . . sir.'

'If you haven't any questions, then, you must know it all. That right?'

There really wasn't much point in carrying on this conversation. I had enough workshop psychology to grasp that I was being used as a kind of stooge – a ventriloquist's dummy, something to bounce smart remarks off, a kind of sounding board to bounce off. Very sage and profound utterances indeed. I thought: 'Go ahead, Yank. It's your show.' Each instructor was allotted two American cadets and two RAF. One of the Americans was called Sanders. He was of indeterminate age, but he made no secret of the fact that he had been married three times. 'I'm like Jesus,' he boasted. 'I love 'em all.' Childers, the other American, was a tall, slim, unremarkable youngster.

The last of the four, Hallaway, had an Asian background of some kind – Malaya, Singapore or some such. In all my experiences, I'd never seen a look of such unalloyed hero-worship as Hallaway shone on our instructor Meryl. He gazed on him wide-eyed and open-mouthed, drank in his every word, and I declare he almost fluttered his eyelids at him. As Wacker Wright said some days later: 'If your instructor ever steps backwards, Hallaway's gonna have some broken fingers.'

Through the window of the flight room, I could see the long rows of biplanes parked wing-tip to wing-tip, some of them being spluttered into life by the students with those massive cranks (rather like the winches on old-fashioned wells). Then away they would go, bumping and 'essing' over the rutted turf to the other side of the field for takeoff. Soon I too would be soaring aloft, above and beyond the sordid machinations of mortal man. The instructor had been droning on (I was not, until later, aware that this also was our instructor's first day, and I suppose he also was having 'new boy' feelings).

Again came the inevitable: 'Any questions?'

My attention had been marginally drawn to a notice tacked on the opposite wall: 'Students will not remain in the cockpit while the A/C is being gassed.' Now 'gassing' was not beyond my comprehension. If a man wanted to gas himself, he usually found a nice bulky cushion, spread it in front of the opened gas-stove door, turned on the taps, and made himself comfortable. Britain had issued gas masks by the million in order to protect people from the ill-effects of gas.

Is it some kind of death-wish that prompts me to lead with my chin? 'Why do aircraft have to be gassed?'

A cloud seemed to have wiped the colour from the airfield, while inside, Meryl Vinter's face seemed to smoulder. When he eventually got his vocal cords into action, he did so to the effect that if any student wanted to be smart, he should wait until he was airborne; and, from all appearances, he looked forward to that with what amounted to lewd relish. Alec Forbes, the chief administrator of the school, had been hovering over the various groups, and now cut in.

'I guess some of you British boys are going to be good and puzzled by some of our terminology. To you most internal combustion engines use petroleum or petrol for fuel. To us that's gasoline, or just gas. Got it?'

I got it, and thanked him, embarrassed all to hell. Vinter also looked uncomfortable. The little bit of terminological interplay had done neither of us any good. Soon afterwards, we were starting up the A/Cs and waddling off to do our 'circuits and bumps', but there was noticeably some lack of happy communion between my instructor and myself.

The ground instructors were obviously teachers from small colleges who had taken short courses in navigation, theory of flight, etc., and they now passed it on, dead-pan and parrot-fashion. There was no spite or malice about these guys. No life either. There was nothing here to fear except falling out of our desks in deep slumber, which wouldn't have been nice. Often the bell would ring for a change of period, leaving me wondering at what part of the lecture I had dozed off. However, with regard to marks and progress, I remained steadily in the centre of the pack.

On the second day, it was announced that certain cadets were to receive immediate, temporary, unpaid promotion. Johnnie Hopwood would be Squadron Leader, Arnold Gates and George Fielding would be flight lieutenants, Doc Davidson and Frank Farley sergeants. This was apparently in accordance with the American forces' cadet system. A similar number of the American students were given the equivalent rank. Nothing to it, really, but it was no added amenity to be marched everywhere by some immature kid yelling: 'Lip ripe, Lip ripe.'

Meryl was not the easiest man to fly with – he tugged and tore at the controls. I began to gather bruises on the insides of my legs where he tugged the stick sideways, normally with the yelled admonition: 'Loosen up! Loosen up!' This then, it would seem, is the approved method of ensuring that the student is thoroughly relaxed. He made no attempt to make his instructions clear. Mostly I had to hazard a guess whether he wanted a slow roll or forced landing procedure. On the second time up, he was giving me 'climbing turn' instruction, how you

41

led with the stick until the guy-wire rested along the horizon and then kept her there with the rudder.

'If you take her too steep, this is what happens,' and he rolled the plane on to her back. I felt myself sliding out of the seat belt, which was loosely draped around my shoulders. I tried to cling on to the sides of the cockpit with my knees (I had a nasty strained feeling in my groin for days afterwards). Just as it was about to slide out of my reach, I grabbed the speaking-tube and yelled: 'You've got her, sir.' In that moment I happened to glance up into the mirror above the front seat and mister bloody Vinter was killing himself with laughter. I instantly managed a laugh of my own (however contrived). I wasn't going to have that bastard aware of how uncomfortable and ridiculous I felt, dangling out of an aircraft that was upside down . . . was I, hell. He'd never be aware of the dark-brown feeling that began to assert itself at the back of my neck . . . would he, hell. He kept her in a laboured inverted climb until the blood felt it was going to burst from my ears. Then he completed the roll.

On the fourth trip, I began to sense that I was going solo. It seemed to be the accepted thing with these Yanks that when a student was ready to 'go it alone', they psychologically tore him to shreds. The normal ranting and raving was increased in tempo. The plane was thrown around in the sky like they wanted to destroy it. My guy was average or worse. He rapidly changed from a shrieking dervish to a deranged psychopath, and then the throttle lever was pushed closed. 'Forced landing,' he yelled. This time I guessed right. I rammed the stick forward to maintain flying speed, and luckily I was able to spot a suitable field straightaway. I side-slipped her down, cleared a low fence, and settled her among the stubble, as light as fairy floss.

'I'm going to get out now and do some figuring,' he said. 'You take her around on your own for a bit, and come and pick me up in twenty minutes.' As part of his normal attire, he was wearing his long, flowing white silk scarf, as became Red Barons and other 'Lords of the Air'. It was this scarf that determined (twenty minutes later) my approach pattern. Wordless and looking disagreeable, he climbed into the cockpit and pointed toward the airfield.

The next day was Saturday, cold and gloomy. 'See if you

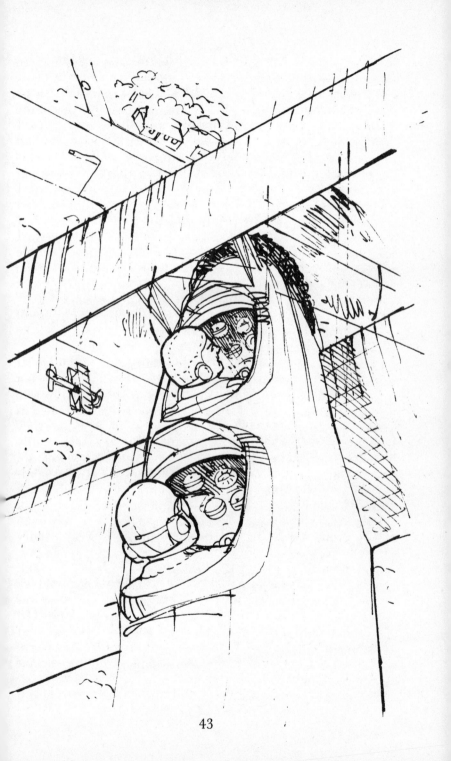

can find a hole in the cloud, and if so,' instructed Vinter, 'do some simulated landings on cloud.' I found a hole in the cloud and climbed through it; then all hell let loose. There were planes zooming, diving and banking around me from every angle. I went through a series of aerobatics I'd never even dreamed of, in order to avoid a dozen or more mid-air collisions. An hour later (hardly able to believe the feel of solid ground beneath me) I was on my way to supper when I was overtaken by half a dozen of the young fry.

'Was that you in 207, Dixie? It was? Ye gods, did we have fun.' Not much point in disillusioning these kids or adding a sour note to the conversation, not a bit of use. I put the laughing mask back on. In the cafeteria one of the instructors approached us and asked if we would like to go to Sunday School the next day. He had to be kidding. No, he wasn't kidding. To break the embarrassing silence, 'I wouldn't mind going to church,' I ventured.

'What denomination are you?'

'Church of England.'

'That's Episcopalian out here. Be at the gate at ten thirty. There will be cars there to pick you up and drive you in.'

It was a nice, white church with a green roof and a small, green spire in a shady, well-kept part of town. The opening hymn was familiar. Halfway through it, a hand reached alongside mine to share my hymn book. It was Kratz's hand, and Kratz was on the end of it. I looked at him quizzically. He smiled and shrugged and went on singing. I waited for him outside the lich-gate.

'Well?'

'Oh, I just like to sing, old horse.'

'Cut it out. What are you up to?'

'Well, I've had an interesting morning.'

'I'm glad.'

'Yes, old horse. I got up early and went down to the depot to the jolly old Santa Fe Railroad. There was a railway coach there, just like the one we travelled in from Kansas City. Just like it. The same high gloss enamelled ceiling. You could lay right back, the way that Farley was doing that morning, and use the ceiling as a mirror. I'm hoping I misjudged you, old horse. Meanwhile, that lady over there with the large beige hat has just asked me if you and I would join her family for lunch.

44

Shall we? Wouldn't it be super if it turned out to be kosher?'
He grinned.

We made our way across the lawn to where our host, hostess, and their Packard were waiting. Their names were Elmer and Alene Boles and, the introductions completed, we were soon rolling down a shady, tree-lined avenue to their home. It felt good to be in home-like surroundings again, except that by all reasonable standards this was lavish. Everything was there and to spare: no apparent regard for cost, the lush plentifulness so obviously taken for granted. Larry wanted to spend the balance of the day looking the town over, but I told him, I had to get back. I had some studying to do.

'Don't you?'

'No, old horse. I don't have to study. I have a photographic memory. Not anything I'm particularly proud about. Something I was born with – could have been three ears. The fact remains that I could repeat those lectures word for word. Never need to take notes.'

'So,' I said as the bus bumped us back to the airfield. 'The course is a snap, eh?'

'Unfortunately, I wouldn't put it quite that optimistically.'

'No? What's the problem then?'

'Air sickness, mostly.'

'And running into this officer cadet thing?'

'Yep, and that too.'

'Marvellous the working of the American mind, ain't it. They seem all agog to give stripes to somebody – anybody. Right? That seems to be the striking difference between the British and the Yanks. We venerate things, they worship people – you know, persons. A nation of hero-worshippers; and if there's nobody around worthy of their adulation, they'll create someone. They get a perfect dog's-body and either give him bloody great stripes on his sleeves or scrambled egg round his hat. They're just bursting to salute someone.'

'Apart from that, how are you making out, Dixie?'

'Well, it's just about like the curate's egg – it's good in parts. Curiously enough, I've come to enjoy flying. Originally I only went into the pilot racket because I was convinced that the side that had the best air effectiveness would be the side that would win. I know we are going to win, eventually, and it sure would burn my arse if I should meet an ex-flyer after the war and have to acknowledge that he did it for me. The average guy only gets the chance of one righteous war. "So stand back, ladies and gentlemen, and let the dog see the rabbit".'

'You're still beating out the same tune, old horse. And you like to fly?'

'Well, it's not the flying that gets me. Mostly that's a disagreeable experience. No, I get a bang out of being able to fly. The first time my instructor put us into a spin, I was scared witless. Yesterday, without any threats or coercion, I went up to seven thou' and did three – two to port and one to starboard, and they came out perfect.'

'So, where's the problem or problems?'

I had to consider for a minute. Was I manufacturing difficulties? Was my apathy toward the States associating itself with the conditions at the airfield? I thought not.

'One of them is the dispatcher.'

'Not our bog-ridden Betty?'

'Yep. The first time I clapped eyes on her, I allowed my evaluation of her to show through. You can't do that and get away with it, Kratters. Those females of the species will get even every time. It never pays to let a woman know that you think she's the pig's rear. In the first place, it's not nice; and the second, it's asking for trouble. On top of which it is all too obvious that my instructor doesn't find her in the least repulsive.'

'You mean there's something going on? What a combination. Dixie old horse, if you'll allow me to say so, YOU'RE DICING WITH DEATH.'

A shiver ran down my back. 'Cut that out, you young prawn. Don't you realize that your race has produced more prophets than human beings?'

'And their batting average,' laughed Kratz, 'is just about as low as they go. They were the first group to establish a "minus" credit rating.'

'So, what's your difficulty? Air sickness, you say. Do you mean you actually throw up in the kite?'

'No, but I sure as hell feel I want to. Do you get a regular stabbing sensation build up in a tight turn?'

'No, and if I did I would seriously consider going on sick call. Why don't you?'

'I think I would, old horse, if I was entirely convinced that the problem is physical. It might not be.'

'What else?'

'Emotional, maybe.'

'You?'

'Well, I have been a bit out of my stride lately. As you know, my bed space is opposite our friend Farley. And you know the inflexible layout of our bed and kit each day.'

'Yeah, I know. The top sheet to be folded back at an angle of sixty degrees, the blanket tucked in so tight that you can drop a penny on it and catch it as it bounces. I suppose that comes under the heading of discipline. I don't see how you can turn a non-flying man into a flyer without laying on a certain amount of bull. This don't bother you none, does it?'

'No, but I've been put on report three times last week for having a lousy bed space. Three times!'

'Well, you'll have to give your stuff a bit more attention of a morning.'

'Dixie, somebody louses up my layout while I'm away. Oh, I'm sure I'm right. My photographic recall. Get me? I know just how things are when I leave. It's just that some mischievous bastard alters them a bit. Not a lot. Just enough to get me into disfavour on a regular basis.'

'Kratters, that sure sounds like a problem situation. Do you think it's that what's giving you the pain in the gut?'

'It could. How can I be sure?'

'Go on sick call and let the sawbones have an opinion.'

'I might at that. What makes you think that Meryl and Betty are hitting it off?'

'Instinct – and observation, young Kratters. When a guy wears fur-trimmed goggles, even inside a building, he's on the prowl. Right? When Meryl comes back to the flights after lunch, he dawdles around and then goes into the instructors' room. Betty surveys the situation immediate and pending, and then hits on some urgent reason to check on something in the instructors' room. On the count of five, the door is slammed shut. Some time later, out comes Betty, tucking her blouse into her skirt-waist, trying not to look ruffled. They quite obviously don't give a damn what the students observe or think. You can't beat a winning hand, can you?'

'True. But you don't seem to have anything really positive to go on, do you?'

47

'Well, have you noticed what happens at the end of day flying? There's nearly always an aircraft to be tested after work has been done on it in the hangar. Who gets to do the testing? Meryl with Betty along for good measure. He belts along, full throttle, for the airfield perimeter, and just as he is running out of time, he drags her into a beautiful steep bank. Ten minutes later, they're back; and a quarter of an hour later, you can spot his bright yellow convertible parked in the Cozy-boy Motel. Now wouldn't that be curious? Meryl doesn't live there.'

'Oh, well, rather him than me.'

'How are you making out with the Yankee students?'

'OK, I guess. They are different though, aren't they. Good God yes.'

'In what way?'

'If I was to describe them in one word, I'd say "glib". They don't seem to have any wall of reserve of any kind. Can you imagine a British airman wandering around a barrack block in a pair of shower sandals and a jockstrap?'

'Not really, and yet there's no logical reason why they shouldn't.'

'None at all. But somehow, they can't seem to stay within themselves. You don't hear an RAF erk announce to the entire room: "I guess I will now study navigation." Who the hell cares what they guess? Give them the slightest opening, and they tell you about their aunt and uncle, who their favourite singer is, who the only baseball pitcher is and then they go off singing *Nothing Can Touch the Army Air Corps*.'

Damn it, Kratters, you're starting to develop a mean, nasty, critical attitude, something similar to mine. I shall be night flying on Tuesday. Can I borrow your camera?'

'Sure. I'll bring it round.'

'And remember to go on sick report tomorrow.'

'I might. Good night.'

4

For night flying, I think in consideration of people of Jackson City who liked to sleep at night, we used a relief landing field about ten miles out. A string of goose-necked flares were set out. At sundown, they gave off a weird, uncertain illumination. I found the whole thing confusing. The exercise was 'circuits and bumps'. Not too difficult, I guess, but it was to me. I always seemed to be all set to land when some other 'bod' was all set to take off. The taxiing around to the takeoff point was not amusing either. The darkness, except for the goose-necks, was intensely black. The aircraft carried no lights. Toward the end, Meryl strode over to me.

'What time do you have?'

'Just an hour and forty minutes, sir.'

'Hell, I'm not interested in that. What time have you got?'

'Do you mean my total time?'

He asked the same damned thing of a Yankee student standing close by, and he looked at his watch and said: 'Eight minutes after two, sir.'

Soon after that, the field became too dusty and flying was scrubbed. We had just completed a circuit when we received the signal to return to base. I joined the traffic pattern and landed.

'Sit tight, and let me have her,' said Meryl.

'You've got her, sir.'

Instead of taxiing around the perimeter, he went careening across the airfield and came to a jolting stop close to the crew room. After I stowed my chute and flying suit, I was making my way toward bed when I had to pass a public pay phone. Meryl was waiting there.

'Do you have any change?' he asked. I did. I changed him a dollar and I soon heard coins clattering into the phone just before I was out of earshot. 'Hello, Betty!'

'Stupid bugger,' I thought. 'If he wanted to know the time, why couldn't he say: "What's the time"?'

I wrote to Eve on every second day, and I couldn't hit the hay until I'd told her how wonderful everything was. I shaded a desk lamp and got cracking.

Our dormitory or barrack block was an H-type structure: two long wings joined in the centre by washrooms, toilets and showers. On Wednesday morning (as those who flew after midnight were excused parade and morning lectures) I lay in my bunk and heard the 'unexcused' clatter out of the door. I got up and twisted a towel round my shoulders and sauntered off to the showers. Wacker Wright was there with his old-fashioned shaving gear, laying a deep layer of soap on his stubble.

'How you doing, Dixie?'

'Bloody horrible. How about you?'

'Oh, san fairy anne,' and as he harvested his whiskers he gave vent to one of his inexhaustible repertoire:

> A strange bird, the cuckoo (Scrape, scrape)
>   He sits on the grass, (Scrape, scrape)
> His wings neatly folded, (Scrape, scrape)
>   His beak up his arse.
> From this strange position (Scrape, scrape)
>   He seldom does flit,
> For it's hard to sing cuckoo (Scrape, scrape)
> 'With a beak full of shit.

In the shower I was in a good position to watch the entrance. Before long Farley came in and sauntered toward Kratz's bunk. I levelled Kratz's camera over the top of the shower partition and click!

'What the hell's going on?' Farley wanted to know.

Wacker said: 'I can't stand these farts who will insist on getting into the picture. Can you, Dix?'

'I sure as hell can't,' I asserted, locking the camera in my locker.

Did Farley realize that the opposition to his machinations was resourceful and practical? Kratz certainly gave him a clean bill of health from then on.

What had been established during my first days at Number 15 BFTS unfortunately did not abate or reverse itself. Vinter never lost an opportunity of belittling and degrading me, and the dispatcher always had me down on her list as the last to fly. I am now, and always was, fully aware that a most damning and dangerous thing in a pilot is confidence. Unless comfortably insecure, you're not going to last. Sure I knew that, and I wasn't a dreamy-eyed kid either. Those safety features and tiresome drills, I adopted, I synchronized to. All in a good cause. I didn't want to be anything but the best. Then returning one day from what I considered an unblemished exercise, I was amazed and disconcerted when Vinter began to berate me solidly and remorselessly about not keeping a continual check, both outside and inside the cockpit. 'One of these days you're going to kill somebody,' he kept repeating. I was puzzled. I didn't get it. Then I found that Wilbur Nye was standing just behind me. What a thoroughly American thing to do. Vinter, in order to improve and boost his own worth in the eyes of the establishment, had to tear me to rags. Who knew such things could have a direct bearing on the future. Who knew!

My seventh week was the kind you like to look back on, knowing it can happen only once. I started off with an 'instrument cross-country'. These could be fun. They were certainly some measure of one's proficiency. After pre-flight cockpit drill the hood was clamped tight, shutting out all visual contact with the outside world. The little group of instruments were my only link with the roaring, wobbling world outside. I made a smooth takeoff and climbed on pattern to 2,000 feet. I then flew at that height across the centre of the airfield, checked the time carefully and, continuing to climb, set course on what was scheduled to be a three-and-a-half-hour trip. After approximately two hours, the hood was sent back with a snap. Bright, brilliant daylight flooded everywhere. (Bright as a clear day can be on the earth's surface, it cannot compare with the brilliant light that you get at height.)

'Are you on course?' Vinter wanted to know. I hurriedly checked my flight plan and map. Sure I was on course. Everything was going 'wizard'.

'Yes,' I said.

'Eh?' he said.

51

'Yes, we're on course,' and I gave him the thumbs-up sign.

'Are you going to stay on course?'

Well, right at that moment I thought it was an unarguable thing to do. After all I had been flying blind for two hours, and we were right over the spot where I had calculated we should be and right on time.

'Yes.'

Vinter nearly went crazy. He seethed; he boiled; he exploded. 'If you don't alter this son-of-a-bitching course, so help me I'll throw you over the side with my bare hands.'

It was then that I noticed a slight darkening of the sky ahead.

'Altering course thirty degrees to port, sir.' It might have been a slight rain squall. This Vinter was not going out of his way to be a pal, certainly.

I got quite a bang out of 'Lazy Eights.' It was an exercise which was carried out over a road intersection. With a good stiff wind blowing, the object was to fly a path through the air, describing a figure eight, the intersection of the figure to correspond exactly with the intersection of the road below. This called for a certain feel for and a mastery over the aircraft. The wind was always a decided yet unpredictable force. It had the ability to nullify your well-considered plans and to thwart your best endeavours. Here was the relentless struggle that would never be won as long as man was determined to fly. I knew I was good at Lazy Eights. I think Vinter did too. As I was about to take off on one of these exercises, he said with a look at the sky: 'If the wind stiffens up, try some "power-on" landings' (that is, instead of shutting off the throttle and stalling into a three-point landing, you use power into the wind and touch down with the front wheels only). The wind picked up considerably, so I carried out the eight power-on landings. I felt good about them. Afterwards, I was met by the chief instructor.

'We thought we were going to have to shoot you down,' he said.

'After I had found my voice, 'I can't think why,' I said.

'Well, goldarn it, you seemed to have forgotten how to bring one in. What was the problem?'

'No problem. Just power-on landings.'

'Never heard of 'em.'

'Well, sir, my instructor was here. Why didn't you check with him?'

'We did, and he said he couldn't think what in hell you were up to.'

'Well I'll be fucked.'

'What was that again?'

I said: 'Forget it, sir.'

The message began to sink in. If I was to make a good pilot, it would not be because of Vinter but in spite of Vinter. A chilling thought. I'd never been actively disliked before.

That night, in the barrack block, the younger fry whooping and zooming around and thrilling one another their day's flying adventures, one said: 'I did a wizard loop today.'

'Oh, so did I! Aren't they great? I like them better than spins.'

'Just how do you do these loops?' I enquired, wondering why my beloved instructor had never sprung them on me.

'Nothing to them, Dixie. You just clear yourself, ease the stick into a shallow dive, wait till you tachometer reaches 2,000 revs, and then tug back on the stick. It's a piece of cake.'

I resolved to try them next day, and I did. I went to the requisite seven thou', checked for other traffic, lowered the nose to a gliding attitude, and when the tachometer read 2,000 revs, I hauled the stick back into my gut and hung on. The little aeroplane roared in protest. Perhaps I blacked out a little. I know I lost 6,000 feet very rapidly, and the whole manoeuvre didn't seem right somehow. I mentally checked the instructions that the small fry had passed along. Nothing seemed to be missing or complicated, so I went up aloft and tried again. The same blasted thing. I decided to leave them for the time being.

That night I hashed the thing around in the barrack room.

'But Dixie, when you were over on your back, didn't you cut your motor?'

'No, you stupid little clot. You didn't say anything about cutting any motor.'

The next day I did them in the approved fashion; when upside down I cut the power, allowing the weight of the engine to take us into a snug little curl and still remain at height.

That was the day I 'ground-looped'.

I had seen several of these ungraceful and destructive manoeuvres and had been secretly congratulating myself that I

could observe these wretched-looking students without emulating them. To explain, – the Steerman has a narrow undercart: that is, the space between the front wheels is less than six feet. In taxiing over rutted mud or uneven turf, it is hardly surprising that these birds do tend to finish up resting on one wing – a ground-loop.

The fabric of the starboard wing was grazed. An accident report had to be formalized. I had been at fault. The instruction was most insistent: if the plane tilts, the throttle must be activated immediately so as to increase the airflow over the control surfaces. The instant I felt her wobble, I was facing a line of picketed aircraft a dozen feet away, so I stood on the brakes.

The mishap was entered into my documents in red ink. The disciplinary outcome was that I had to walk twice around the perimeter of the airfield wearing inner and outer flying suits, flying boots and helmet, three pairs of gloves, with my parachute clumping into the backs of my calves. During this entire journey I was to use my right hand, simulating the opening of a throttle: all rather childish and hilarious, but nobody laughed. It was a sweltering day, and days can be sweltering in June in Oklahoma. After I had completed the second lap, I managed to shrug off with a grin the chirpings of sympathy that greeted me.

The next day I was returning from the post office at lunch time when Wilbur Nye fell into step beside me.

'Where are you bound for this afternoon, Mr Day?' he asked, clumsily ingratiating.

'Oh, just a routine cross-country hop: Clearwater, Hominy, and Schiedler way.'

'Now that sounds right fine. If I can clear up my paperwork, I'll see if I can come along with you just for the ride.'

Blast! There goes the chance of a bit of easy flying, I thought. This malarkey about paperwork wouldn't deceive a day-old infant. He was going to check me out. I must get airborne before the paperwork is cleared up. Vinter met me at the locker-room door.

'Wilbur Nye says he will fly with you this afternoon. Here, just a minute. You can't wear this. It's soaked through still; it would freeze like a board up there.'

'It will be OK, thanks,' but it was drenched with perspiration from the previous day.

'Here, put this on quick. Wilbur's waiting.' He tossed me over a sheepskin sidecut. After protesting, I gave in and struggled into it. It fit me all right, but the sleeves seemed tight.

Nye was waiting at the side of the roaring plane. Had I got the flight plan? Had I got the map with the various courses marked on? Had I marked on the five and ten degree lines? 'OK, take her off then.'

It wasn't a bad day for flying: about four-tenths cumulus cloud, the air comfortably fresh with enough air pockets to make it a ride rather than a journey. I climbed out of the circuit and flew into wind for about five miles. Then, as per procedure, I backed round to pass over the airfield on course and log the time. Time is the most essential element in navigation. There were no clocks in the Steerman console. No big deal. I had a watch which I always used. But my watch was on my upper wrist; the flying jacket was extraordinarily tight at the wrists and I had gauntlets on. I held the stick with my knees and gave that watch problem some attention.

'Do you always fly one wing low?'

'No, sir. My watch is . . . .'

'Well, fly the plane, God damn it. I can't hear what you're saying. Are you on course? Eh? Just look at your air speed. I can't hear what you're saying. When are you going to flatten out?'

'Sir, I'm trying to get my watch.'

I thrust my hand out of the cockpit and pointed to my wrist.

'How in hell do you expect to fly a God-damned plane waving your arms? Fly the plane, mister. I can't hear what you're saying.'

According to my logbook, the trip took one-and-a-half hours; the dialogue never varied. Then, miraculously, for I was completely lost, came deliverance. The patchy cloud which had been swatting at us made a kaleidoscope of dun-coloured meaningless patterns on the ground. Then I saw in the far distance a tiny patch of highly illumined ground, made so by a complete break in the cloud. It could have been a mirage, but it seemed to me that in that minute patch of landscape was the suggestion of a river and what could have been a railway bridge crossing it. I banked round.

'Changing course to two-nine-oh degrees, sir,' and that was

it. I completely ignored the ravings of the guy up front. I resisted manually the wrenching of the controls. I joined the home-base circuit, landed, and parked the aircraft. Wilbur Nye was a while coming around the tail to me. He was examining the ground when he gritted out: 'The takeoff and landing were good, but what in tarnation went on in between?'

'I really don't think you want to know, sir. You didn't trouble to find out up there, did you. A good dozen times you yelled: "I can't hear what you're saying." Why the hell was that? You had earphones on your headset, as I did. How is that you didn't want to know up there? But as you've asked me, I'll tell you what went on. You, sir, went into your cheap, nauseating little tough-guy routine, your sadistic little act. Around fifteen times you said you couldn't hear what I was saying. Why couldn't you hear? You had a headset and earphones the same as I had. You Americans seem to spend half your time trying to impress the world how tough, wise, and righteous you are. You don't hesitate to ram it down people's throats with anything that's handy – with an aircraft, if necessary. You wasted your time with that little performance this afternoon. I was not impressed.' With that I tugged off the sidecut, threw it on the instructor's desk, and walked past Wilbur and out of the door.

He was spluttering. 'Now lookit here now.' I didn't pause or look back.

The evening that followed was not a happy one for me. Smouldering fits of rage followed bouts of self-pity and self-disgust. True I should not have found myself in that rotten situation on the trip. But why had I been bloody stupid enough to point out to a Yank what his shortcomings were? All the studying, all the hours of square-bashing, all the cross-country running had been blown. I knew I had kissed my flying career goodbye: all that solid effort down the pan.

I ambled around to Larry's billet. Wacker Wright was holding forth to a crowd of American students. They were interested in British royalty.

'Have you ever seen the King, Wacker?' one of them wanted to know.

'Well, yes, I've seen him, several times, though they normally keep him under wraps and you have to stand in a queue (sorry, chaps, I mean a line-up) and watch His Nibs drive past

57

the end of it. Since the start of the war, though, he's been going to a lot of munitions works and airfields. I've heard a yarn that's going around that he was handing out gongs (sorry again, chaps, that means he was awarding decorations). There were about ten of these fighter pilots lined up, and His Majesty was pinning DFCs to their tunics and reading the citation as he went. He got to one of these shy, modest recipients who was waiting there with his chest stuck out a foot.

"I must c-c-congratulate you, S-S-Squadron Leader, for personally shooting down t-t-two Junkers, th-th-three MEs, and f-f-four Fokkers."

'The fighter type says: "No, excuse me, Your Majesty, that should be five Fokkers."

'The king looked down his citation list. "F-f-four Fokkers." The fighter type was a stubborn bastard, not very bright, and maintained that it should read five Fokkers until the king finally looked him in the eye and remarked: "S-S-Squadron Leader, I don't give a damn whether it was f-four Fokkers or f-five Fokkers, you're only getting one fucking medal".'

☆   ☆   ☆

'You are looking at a fighter type who is never going to be a threat to the Hun,' I told them.

'Why? What's happened?'

So I related the sordid chain of events that occupied the afternoon.

'You're in the shit, Dixie,' averred Larry.

'In the shit up to your adenoids,' seconded Wacker.

'It's a doggoned pity you didn't know about that tight wristband routine,' said Olson, one of the American boys in the advanced flight. 'They try and use it all the time.'

'Do you mean it's a pre-arranged drill?'

'Yep.'

'So, regardless of what I did this afternoon, I was still due for the chop?'

'Well, what other way could you work it? There's 300 of us here under training, and a handful of civilian types. What other way could you maintain order except by the constant threat of the boot. Five per cent of every intake go that way. I've noticed that it's not the poor flyers or the slow ones in class, but usually from the middle of the pack.'

It was some comfort to see the concern and sympathy reflected in their eyes. Larry was on his feet, giving my shoulder a friendly pounding.

'But for heaven's sake, don't do anything, Dixie. You'll only make matters worse.'

'How in hell's name could things be worse? I think I remember telling you that anyone who screwed me up on this course did so at their peril. Right now, I'm going over to the locker room. I'll find the tight-wristed jacket and ease it out with my jack-knife – just to let these bastards know that I'm on to them.'

'We'll come with you.'

'Like hell you will . . . but thanks. I'll manage.'

5

The 'sword of Damocles' hovered and wavered but did not fall.
I needed another seven hours of solo flying to complete my
elementary course, after which we were to go on a week's leave.
The unholy partnership of Meryl and Betty, which I secretly
referred to as 'the bedmates', arranged to have my name at the
bottom of the list for the day's flying. This meant that I would
spend the whole of a flying period 'winching' the engines on the
other guys' planes and seeing them bumping off to the takeoff.
Often by the time I was allocated a plane, the control tower
would fire off a red Very light to indicate an end to the day's
flying. At this time, Meryl and Betty would laughingly stroll
out to an aircraft that was ready for testing. He followed the
same procedure all the time: roaring full-throttle over the
airfield, almost touching it, and then at the boundary pulling
her into a tight banking turn. I longed for the flukey breeze to
be there, just enough to drag that wing-tip in the dirt. After the
test flight, they would pile into Meryl's yellow convertible and
roar away to the Van Winkle motel. I, on the other end of the
scale, would trudge back to the billet, dusty, sweaty, tired,
depleted and thoroughly 'brassed off'.

At the close of one such afternoon session, I heard my name.
It was the voice of my beloved dispatcher snarling: 'Day, 207's
coming in. Go fly.'

I hefted my parachute and went out to meet the plane which
was essing towards the picket line.

'Don't switch off,' I shouted.

'Why not?' enquired Duckworth, the student who was
bringing her in.

'I'm taking her up.'

'I wouldn't.'

'Why?'

'The son of a bitch won't fly, that's why. Bugger-all power. Don't climb worth a damn. I wouldn't take the piss-begotten thing up.'

'Well, I just want to get a half-hour in before they scrub flying for the day.'

'It's up to you.'

The aircraft changed hands, and I trundled it over to the takeoff point as fast as I could.

With one eye on the control tower, I turned her into the wind and gradually pressed forward the throttle lever. She was slow to respond. I pressed the throttle open to the fullest extent, but she wasn't gaining much speed. I lifted the tail wheel off: no perceptible increase in speed. Was the grass taller and thicker on this strip of field? The grasses seemed to be clinging to the wheels. 'Git on, girl!' I applied a light backward pressure on the stick. We wallowed briefly into the air and then the under-cart was once more jostling the grasses. We were more than half-way across the field now, way past the point of no return. We were moving remorselessly towards the hangars. They came nearer, increased in height. 'Come on, old lady, up you go! Get up, you rotten bitch!' We were airborne now, the hangars a hundred yards ahead with eighty feet more altitude than we had got. What to do: try to turn away from the hangar? With our little piddling fifty-five knots, we'd side-slip into the deck. If I tried to touch down and brake, I should bury her nose into the foot of the building. 'come on, girl, try.' Sometimes you can notice a slight pressure differential when flying over a hill, a clump of trees even. That's what we got, and it just barely allowed us to scrape over the hangar roof. 'Oh! You sweetheart. You made it.' I nursed a little more height out of her and then was content to put in time. Then I turned back to the field and commenced landing procedure. As I did so, I was shocked to see that I had only one bank of magnetos switched on.

What the hell was wrong with me? How could I be so utterly irresponsible? A pre-flight cockpit check would have shown me the lethal situation we were in. But I hadn't done a pre-flight cockpit check, had I? I badly needed my arse kicked. How could I? I knew then how it had come about: I had been so concerned with getting that damned kite off the ground before flying was scrubbed. If that benighted dispatcher had given me time like the other guys were getting, I shouldn't find myself taking these rotten short-cuts. To hell with those blasted 'bedmates'. They were fast becoming a fantasy with me. I could trace any and every untoward happening to them, individually or collectively.

So came the last day before leave. Many of the students had already completed their flying hours and were busy getting their suitcases and haversacks ready for their trips. Some were going south; mostly they were content with Kansas City as their destination.

Larry was going to New York. 'Come with me, Dix.'

'Fat chance. I still have another three-and-a-half hours to get in. I shan't be through by six o'clock' (the Streamline Express went through at five-thirty).

'Well, if you get the chance, get yourself a bed at the New York USO and leave a message at the stage-door canteen.'

'See you,' I said. Come to think of it, I never did see Larry again.

I now had the entire chunk of air to myself. The weather was warm and sunny with a light freckle of cirrus cloud at about forty thou'. Nothing to bother me. I was just stooging around when I noticed the shadow of my plane coasting along in the river far below. I orbited and put myself in a position so that the plane's shadow and the river appeared together at the root of my port wing. The wing hid the violent turns and twists the river was to make, and in order to keep my plane's shadow within the river's bank, I had to do some nifty manoeuvring. I got quite fascinated by this little game, and in following it I must have improved my co-ordination and general flying airmanship 100 per cent. I watched, from above, my buddies boarding the Streamline Express. Soon after, the sun began to dip low on the horizon and the air cooled off. When I finally landed, balanced my logbook, and had grabbed myself a sandwich, it was seven o'clock. I passed the Van Winkle motel and saw the bright yellow convertible parked outside and gave it a silent blessing.

Soon thereafter I was on the road with my thumb at the ready. There was not a great volume of traffic on the road. Mostly the lifts I got were from farmers and tradesmen. Nice people all, but not the adventurous types that would go for an evening's spin of 200 or 300 miles. Darkness was descending

and the air was chilly. I had noticed some dark objects along
the surface of the highway. I struck a match and examined one.
They were rattlers. They were about eighteen inches long and
quite dead, having tried to share the same portion of road with
the day's headlong traffic. Soon afterwards, a blue pick-up
truck slowed down alongside me and I hopped in.

'Turned cold,' observed the driver. 'Going far?'

I told him I was making for Florence.

'You won't make any Florence tonight, you won't.'

'No?'

'Gosh, no. Never see no traffic on this road. Not this late, you
don't. You'd best come home with me, you had.'

'Well, that's extremely kind of you. I'm going to accept now,
in case you change your mind. I'm Arthur Day, by the way.'

'Adam Destry.'

We shook hands. His were huge.

'Are you sure your wife won't be annoyed, springing a
strange man into her house at this time of night?'

'Oh, it's not that late, it ain't. I've still got chores to do. Did
you ever milk a cow?'

'No, but tonight is as good a night as any to learn.'

'Now ain't that the truth, ain't it. I'm helping out while my
brother is at a convention up there in Kansas City. I still have
his cows to milk and his pigs to feed. Shouldn't take long, being
there's the two of us.'

I almost found myself saying: 'Ain't that the truth.'

'We just have another four miles to go on the highway, and
then we strike east for another six. Not bad country seen in the
daylight. Some people call it rattlesnake country. To me it's
black grape country: in another couple of months you'll see all
the hedges loaded with black grapes.'

'You mean they grow wild?'

'They sure as hell do, and they're not the only things that do.
Plenty of turtles. I bet you've never had real turtle soup, eh?
And cows.'

'Now wait a minute. You're not going to tell me you're
going to give me my first milking lesson on wild cows. I know
it's not late, but it's too bloody late for that.'

'You speak a strange lingo. What is it, British or sup'n?'

'Yes, British.'

'You know when I was motoring up behind you, I felt there

63

was something funny about you.'

'And yet you offered me hospitality. Why?'

'Now don't get my wrong. When I say funny I don't mean queer, I don't. I mean unusual. When we graduated from high school, there wasn't one of us who could trace his ancestry back to the British. You're probably the first Brit I've met. Now while we're at it, let me put you right on a couple of things. I've got my own feelings about the war over there. Lots of us around here are still smarting from the depression. If our country can put untold money behind the Brits, where was that money when *we* needed it? If you and I knew the answer to that, we would know why it is I'm not married.'

'And the cows?'

'Now, whatever those cows were once as to their antecedents, they are good cows now. You see, straight east of here we have a length of dual railway line, where the freight trains pull in to let the Streamline Express go by. Sometimes it has to wait almost an hour. While it's there, my brother and I take a walk along the track. Often there's cattle-cars ferrying cattle during the dry spells – to better pasture further north. All right so far? Well, sometimes cows have had calves during the journey. Poor little critters would just get tramped on if left there. So we do our best to get those little buggers out of there, for purely humanitarian reasons, and we find them a home. Look at it this way. We are not stealing nothing. A cow gets on at one end, and a cow gets off at the other end. How can anyone have stolen anything?'

We left the highway and were soon bumping along a dirt road, and presently we saw a light twinkling between trees just away in a hollow, a half-mile from the road.

'That's our place, or rather my brother's place. Mine is two miles further on.'

I had never seen my new-found friend in the daylight. What kind of folk would they be and what kind of a set-up was I walking into? He was almost seven feet tall when he unfolded himself from behind the steering wheel, and I would guess he was a good six years younger than me.

The spread was a pleasant surprise. As we entered the yard, a fluorescent yard-light switched on, showing a modern if modest farmhouse. The yard was relatively clean and smelled only faintly 'farmy'. About fifty feet from the house there was a small, hip-roofed barn, and I could see other lower-set build-ings further back. We went directly to the barn, where Adam switched on the light and started scooping a meagre measure of oats into separate places in the mangers.

'I'll get you the quietest ones,' volunteered Adam.

He went to the barn door and shouted 'Daisy' and 'Rose' and then busied himself putting out more little heaps of oats. Presently I could hear some heavy breathing and then, out of the blackness of night, swung the two nominated cows. They blinked momentarily at the light, at me, and then ignored us both. With a display of single-mindedness, they waddled over to their little pile of oats.

Adam drew a milking-stool up to the port side of Rose and then introduced me to the rather pink and distended equip-ment she had suspended there.

'It's rather like playing a five-finger exercise,' Adam in-structed, 'starting with the index finger and transferring the pressure lightly from one finger to the next.'

I was dog-tired to start with, and I was soon aching from a number of unusual places. Adam was on hand to finish off a cow I had milked and quietly assist them back out of the barn. Another name would be shouted into the night and another warm, businesslike nominee would come swaying in the door and make her way to the small amount of oats. At last the milking was accomplished and the pigs slopped. I followed Adam into the dwelling outhouse to remove our footwear and to wash up.

'Guess what I've brought you from town, Jenny,' sang out Adam through the sitting room.

'Not another diamond necklace? Why, hello!'

When Jenny appeared around the door arch, she was what we cinemagoers were led to expect the modern American housewife to be: slim, light-coloured, neat. She wore a sleeve-less, tan-coloured, linen dress and fluffy mules on her feet. She must have had a mouthful of perfect teeth, but she didn't brandish them. She managed to communicate without much facial expression, dead-pan. When she smiled, it was with a crinkling at the corners of her eyes and the compression of her lips.

She looked into my eyes, with hers twinkling mischief.

'Take him back, Adam.'

'Jenny, I want you to meet Arthur. He's . . . .'

'No, let me guess. He's a serviceman – flyer, maybe. Our boys don't wear that type of cap. Don't tell me he's a Brit. Well now, better come on in. We've got nothing fit for a Brit to eat. We just have a cold supper whenever Adam comes over to do our marketing for us. We never quite know when to expect him. We have several grass widows in town. He's been gone since ten this morning, and all he had to do was change the library books. Getting back to supper: there's some hot soup on the back-burner, if you like turtle soup. If you boys would like to help yourselves, there's a little bit of ham and chicken, and a few tomatoes. Pour yourselves a tumbler of wine.'

'I couldn't find you another Tennessee Williams, but that new number at the library thought you might get by with Hemingway.'

'You get along just fine with the new library gal, uhm?'

'Uhm! Uhm! She was telling me she used to teach school. I bet the boys in her class were dropping pencils all day long.'

'You big dope. You're not supposed to have thoughts like that until you're married, is he, Arthur. Are you married, Arthur?'

Two places had been set for us on a lovely polished oval table, a sturdy flagon of dark wine within easy reach. Jenny protested that she had already eaten and asked to be excused while she leafed through her books. Without looking up, she would give me a mild interrogation, mostly about the blitz. By now, I was too drowsy to answer in more than monosyllables. Adam kept replenishing my glass until the lights started to dim and the small noises seemed to recede into the distance.

Some time later, I heard: 'You're falling off the chair, Arthur. I'd better put you to bed. Lean on me. That's right. This way . . . .'

The bed was clean, comfortable, and somehow welcoming. I groped for my pyjamas in my haversack, but I'm sure I blacked out before I got them on.

'Where's Adam?' I managed to croak, as I experienced the sensation of someone tucking me in.

'He had to leave. You'll see him tomorrow.'

'And the cares that beset the day rolled up their tents like the Arabs and as quietly stole away.'

The morning sunlight was crystal clear through those spotless windows. A lazy breeze gently moved the muslin curtains, and I fell to thoughtful speculation about the wonders of nature: how, for instance, the human spine is composed of numerous small sections, each one denoted at our neck and shoulders by a small bump, each one the right size and the right distance from its neighbour. I had an example of this, about eighteen inches from my nose. The skin covering looked smooth and soft, and I could note not only a few wayward freckles but a few short hairs, gleaming gold from the sunshine. Presently my bed partner rubbed the back of her head vigorously, stretched laboriously, lowered her feet to the floor, sat on the edge of the bed, flipped at a ribbon, and her night attire was soon cascading to the bed. She reached over to a bedside chair, took a beribboned harness from the chair back, and secured it around her waist. She then swirled it around so that the fastenings were at the back, thrust her arms through the ribbon straps, and her breasts somehow disappeared into it. She caught my eye in the mirror.

'You're awake,' she accused.

'I'm afraid so. I'm sorry. I didn't allow you the privacy that the situation called for, but I have a weakness for extending my education.'

'And that's what you were doing?'

'Let's call it that. By the way, what do you call that neat gadget you're wearing?'

'Oh, this? This is called a brassiere, a "bra" to its friends.'

'Oh really?'

'Doesn't your wife wear one?'

'I don't think so.'

'Don't British women wear them?'

'I really don't know, but I don't think so.'

'Perhaps they don't need them.'

'Maybe.'

'I've heard it said, but I don't suppose there's any truth in it, that the British men don't wear jockstraps either.'

I reached up and grabbed her shoulder and flattened her to the bed. Her arms went around my neck as she gripped her chest to mine, so much so that I had to exert considerable pressure so that I could sweep away the material that encased it and take possession of that arrogant breast and sulky nipple.

For the second time that day I returned to consciousness

67

contemplating the muslin window curtains lazily stirring. As my eyes took in their unaccustomed surroundings, a tide of self-disgust permeated my entire being. For a short while, I was able to convince myself that it hadn't happened. It had. The man I now knew I was, was a complete stranger. The man with the code was gone: the man who had stood at the altar rails with Eve and had known he would honour, and keep always, the vows he was making – had gone. I hastily dressed, collected my knapsack, and made for the back door. I had to pass by Jenny, who was bent over the stove, frying eggs. She had a large oval dish on the warming rack with about eight cooked eggs on it.

'Breakfast is ready,' she remarked without looking up.

'No, I'd better be hitting the road.'

'Just as you like,' she said, and slithered the whole plateful of eggs into the garbage.

I patted her shoulder as I passed. 'Thanks, Jenny.'

I clattered over the uneven yard and felt somehow relieved when I was tramping the road again. I had an acrid taste in my mouth and a sensation of some chilling substance seeping through my veins. How dark and foreboding life had suddenly become.

The very real threat that I should not be allowed to finish my course hung over me. That would mean an indefinite posting to Canada, doubtless until the end of the war, however long that might be. To suffer that separation from Eve would be intolerable. Now in addition would be feelings of worthlessness and guilt. Those blasted 'bedmates' were the cause of it all. Without their malevolent manoeuvring, I would have been in New York now, not blundering about in this snake-infested wasteland.

I didn't have to walk far. A milk-tank truck offered me a lift. The driver was collecting milk from various farms, and he was now fully loaded and on his way to Kansas City. The driver was an earnest, good-hearted family man with quaint, simplistic, homespun views. He drove at a steady forty miles an hour. Fast enough – I was going nowhere much. The thoughts that thronged my mind as we bumped along would still be there with me when I alighted. Abe, the driver, was enthusiastic about me going home with him to meet his wife and family. I had to lie my way out of that. Was this to be the pattern of my life now? To lie and to deceive? How else was I to meet Eve eventually? I couldn't hurt her. I couldn't completely disillusion her. Those blasted 'bedmates' had something to answer for.

Kansas City: the wide streets, the background smells of coffee and popcorn, the garish lights, the same tunes played ad nauseam on a dozen and one nickelodoens. I wandered down its streets the next day, still carrying my depression with me. I began to realize that I was being hailed from across the street.

'Hi there, Limey.' Two doughboys were trying to attract my attention. I waved and sauntered on. I heard a galloping of footsteps behind me and caught the reflection, in a store window, of a couple of soldiers in their stupid, demeaning doughboy hats overtaking me.

'So, how are they treating you?' they panted together.

'Oh, can't complain. How are you?'

'So, how are they treating you?' They were pink with embarrassment and quite obviously had friendly intentions. They couldn't be for real, could they? They were on the point of asking me once again how they were treating me, when one had a minor inspiration.

'How do you like the beer?'

I managed to conjure up a puzzled frown. 'What's beer?'

Now they were happy. Here was someone even dumber than they were. Here was someone heaven-sent and ready for an initiation of the most humorous and entertaining kind.

'Eh, do you know what? You're in luck, because there's a bar right along the street from here, and do you know what they sell? BEER. We've just got time to show you.'

With an excited hand at my shoulder-blade, they propelled me along the sun-drenched street, joyously anticipating my introduction to beer. Presently we ducked into a low-pitched establishment where the atmosphere, owing to the aid of modern American air-conditioners, was refreshingly cool. It was comfortable and the lighting was subdued; all the windows were shaded. Ed and Cal almost came to blows trying to decide who should have the honour of buying the three glasses. When they arrived, I toasted them and sank mine half-way down. It was weak and cold, like the sun on an English November morning. My two new friends stood back and watched me speculatively. They told me they were attending a military

69

course and had just stepped out during a 'smoke break' from an instructional classroom close by. I drained my glass and reassured them that the beer was certainly nice and cold and wet and offered to buy the next round. They wouldn't hear of it, and soon replacements were to hand. Cal left for the 'boys' room' and must have somehow suffered a fit of considerable inaccuracy. When he returned, his trousers were badly splashed.

Ed looked at his watch and decided he could just about duck back into class and did so. Cal glanced down at his disaster area and calculated that the odds were considerable against him returning to the fold and rejoining his buddies.

'You know what?' he said. 'There's a bar at the end of the streetcar line, where they sell really good beer.'

This association was beginning to be quite bothersome, but when stubbornly naive people insist on being stubbornly naive, what can you do? We got to the end of the streetcar tracks and found the bar. Cal just managed to finish off his glass of beer and passed out – quite literally passed out. Slapping his face and pouring water over his head failed to have any noticeable effect on him. He surrendered himself completely, and without stint, to Morpheus.

'Hey, barman, this guy's passed out.'

'I know.'

'Is there anything we can do?'

'Nope.'

'Just leave him there snoring?'

'That's what we usually do. He's been here before.'

I couldn't just wander off, leaving the guy out cold, could I? But I did.

The streetcar clattered mile after mile back to the heart of the city, carrying its sole passenger who was asking: 'Do I feel like a heel because I am a heel?' Funny, I'd never been troubled with introspection before.

That afternoon I spent in the saddle.

Yes. About two o'clock, someone drove up to the USO and asked if anyone would like to go horseback riding. Well, thank you very much: I did. We drove a little way out into the country where our mounts were waiting, having thoroughly resolved not to take any nonsense from city folk.

There were five of us. I suppose I was the only one who had

never even been on a rocking-horse. The other four stepped up to their horses with confidence, slapping the sides of their steaming necks, stroking their noses, and talking to them in stern no-nonsense horse talk, which the great animals obviously expected and related to. By Hobson's choice, I was paired off with a tall, wayward-looking thing which kept tossing its head in the air and dismissing with a loud snort my fraternal overtures. At last we were off, the four others walking in 'line astern', mine anxious to prove he could keep up with the others, only sideways. I suppose horses will be horses. My mount did, however, have a disturbing effect on the others and could easily have been an embarrassment. But why should I be embarrassed? I was only sitting on the blasted thing. Our ride took us to the river, which was shallow enough for the horses to splash their way upstream, much to everyone's enjoyment. In avoiding the capering of my mount, the owner of the animals had his hat knocked off and watched as it swirled briefly among the eddies and then sank. There's headgear and headgear. This one must have cost the equivalent of a couple of months of my pay. The owner said it didn't matter, he didn't care, and it was just an old thing that he'd grabbed as he came out. Well, he should know. I noticed, however, as we parked the animals back in their homes and he was asking us to come out again 'real soon', he wasn't looking in my direction particularly.

We had passed a small park on our way. A quiet little oasis kind of place: shady trees, green grass and winding footpaths. Next morning I went back there, armed with half-a-dozen air letters and a topped-up fountain pen. Conveniently there was a picnic table under a tree and I was able to rattle off four passable letters: one for that day, the others at two-day intervals. At lunch time, I found a little eatery just outside the park. After I'd taken on a fried egg sandwich and coffee, I sauntered back to my seat. I had some stiff thinking to do.

There was I, in a foreign land, donkey's miles from the main focus of my existence, and the powers-that-be were determined to bring to a close my valid expectations and aspirations – totally unjustly. I knew in those last four hours of flying that I was a good pilot. I could fly the arse of anything. Hitherto, I had a wary respect for the air and heights. In those last few hours I had developed a kind of brotherly affection for them.

72

They could never dump me from lack of competence in the air, but how could I defend myself in what was truly an indefensible position? I had heard many times that the best defence is attack. That deserved thinking about.

A lazy, but persistent blow-fly had insisted on exploring my head, my hands, my ears. At last I nailed him, and as I looked on his flattened and defeated guck, a feeling of peace stole over me. 'So perish my other enemies.' I rested my head on my arms and heard only distantly and vaguely the sounds of other life.

'Hey, mister! You sleeping or sup'n?' A little lad of about six was rocking my shoulder. He had ridden up to the picnic table on his little three-wheeled bike.

'I'm okay, little man. Just taking a bit of shut-eye.'

'Yeah? My dad used to do that. I used to have to beat him up some.'

'That must have been nice. Real nice.'

'Yeah. And you know what, mister? My dad's coming to visit tonight. An' you know what? He's going to bring me a catcher's mitt.'

'What's that?'

'You know – a catcher's mitt. You a stranger round these parts or sup'n?'

'Yes.'

'No kiddin'. You ever go to the "Neverglades"? Mister, did you ever go to the Grand Canyon? Well, I guess we've sure got a great little ole country right here.'

Having so delivered himself, he set his tricycle in motion.

'Nice meeting you,' he called. 'Any guy can do anything, right here.'

If that small, piddling, pedalling American had allowed me to complete my nap, it would have saved me the embarrassment which was to follow. As I sat there, shaking off the lingering dregs of sleep, I saw coming towards me a pair of sensibly styled shoes. The Cobbler in *Chu Chin Chow* remarked: 'I judge the world by the way they tread.' For a while, I could see only the feet of the young person coming my way. Leafy boughs hid the rest, but what a tale those shoes told. Misery . . . deprivation . . . misfortune. That young person coming around the path had had the course. When she finally came into view, her face matched her seeming fortune: it was colourless and devoid of makeup. It was the kind of face that could have used

73

some. Stray wisps of hair streaked damply about her forehead and ears. She was clad in drab, unattractive clothing. Age? Anywhere from fourteen to nineteen. She was engrossed in her thoughts and had not noticed me until I took a step in her direction.

'Excuse me, miss,' I ventured. 'Are you sure you feel well enough to go on? You look all in. Don't you think you should sit down for a minute?'

I was rewarded by a smile that temporarily lit up her plain and perspiring countenance. She nodded absently and sank on to the seat which I had just vacated.

'Perhaps just for a tiny spell (sigh). It was like a madhouse in there again today. They'd given the night guy the evening off and there was all his stuff. Wait a minute, you're not Marcus, are you? I took you for Marcus, my brother Abe's pal. Well, who are you?'

'Just a foreign soldier on leave.'

'Well now, ain't that swell. Wait till I tell the folks. They've been real interested in soldiers since my two brothers joined up. What way were you going? Our place is only a mile past the park, and I must be getting there. I have the baby to attend to. Why don't you stop in and say hello to the folks? They'll be tickled to death.'

'No, I couldn't do that. I've never met them. Did you say you have a baby at home?'

'Yep, and he's so cute. No, he really is cute.'

'I'm sure he must be. I could walk a little way along the road with you, if you like. You said just now something was a madhouse. What was that?'

'Oh, that was the place where I work: The Seven Seas Restaurant, right there on Main Street. I bet you know it. I'm a dishwasher there.'

'And you don't like it?'

'No, but what's the good of hating it?'

'Why don't you quit?'

'Heavens above! I shall never quit. I shall be there for the rest of my life. When my Pop got me the job, he told them there was no danger of me ever quitting. "She's all yours," he says, "and see to it you don't coddle her none".'

'I'm sure he never meant that.'

'Oh yes, he sure did. I suppose it's like he says: it'll do me

74

good in the long run. After all, I didn't have to go and get myself pregnant, and they haven't abandoned me.'

'No, it doesn't sound as if they have actually gone that far. But where's the baby's father? Isn't he concerned?'

'That's what hurts. That really hurts. He's the boy next door, and all the time he looks the other way. If I'm walking the baby in the back yard when he comes home, he cycles all round the block and goes in at the front. But you'd think, now and then, he would at least be curious about his own kid, wouldn't you, mister?'

'Certainly. But what about friends?'

'Nope. No friends. My Pop says I have sinned, and I gotta pay, and that don't include friends and going to movies and such. And sometimes it seems hard. The kids I went around with, still bobbysoxers, chattering off to school. College pretty soon, some of them I wouldn't wonder. The baby's father among them. I used to cry a lot, but that don't help none.'

During this time I had kept pace with this young person who was hell-bent to see her child. What in hell was I doing here, soaking up misery by the gallon poured out by some little dame I didn't even know?

'Well,' I said, 'this is where we must say goodbye. From what you tell me, your standing with the family is hardly likely to improve by being seen talking to a strange man.'

'You can say that again, though I would have liked you to see the kid. He's so cute. That's where I live, that house on the corner. Oh! help. That's my dad in the yard; he's seen us . . . .'

'In that case, I'll have to do a bit of inventing. Take your cue from me. I'll try and think something up. Compose yourself and walk politely by me.'

I strode past her in at the gate and walked up to the man with my hand outstretched.

'How do you do. I'm from the phrenological survey. I seem to have got my bearings fouled up at the park back there. I was asking this young person if there was any infants under the age of six months around here, and she says there is indeed one right here in this house. In the interest of phrenology, do you mind if I look at your child, sir?'

'The kid ain't mine.'

'He's mine,' said the girl.

'Well, in that case, would *you* mind very much? I would only

75

keep him a minute; and you, sir, I wonder if you'd mind calling me a cab. I'm getting a bit behind with my schedule.'

Amid a good deal of cooing and fussing, a pasty-faced child was produced, dribbling above and steaming below. Its rather large head wobbled unpredictably and precariously on its unsubstantial neck. It was brought out to me into the back yard, where I had taken possession of a rather rickety stool. I had pulled out my pay-book and was elaborately taking notes.

'Now,' I lectured, 'we are only interested in the shape of his head, nothing else you understand. And the fee we pay is precisely one dollar. This infant has no Jewish blood in his veins, has he? Not that there is anything wrong with Jews, but they do have a racial type of bone structure in the skull. This can influence our findings, you understand. You, sir, do you mind holding the child over there just out of the sun and rotating him around slowly as I give you the word? That's it. Primarily we are interested in the set of the ears in relation to the skull, and to a lesser degree the space and level of the eyes. Now, if you could turn the subject round slightly so the back of the cranium is towards me. Excellent! One more view from the top, and we're through. That's it, and thank you sir.'

I closed my pay-book with a snap and replaced it in my breast-pocket with a flourish. 'I suppose you've noticed, sir, the infant shows distinct signs of having very considerable character. Without consulting my tables, I would say his leanings would be towards the geophysical and possibly the archaeological. Give him lots of love and sunshine. And . . . ah, I see my cab has arrived. Thank you all once again.'

I was heartily relieved to be sinking into the upholstery of the cab, and as I did so I glanced back to see the grandfather eyeing that unprepossessing baby with something approaching interest.

Back at the USO, I took myself severely to task. From that point on, I decided, I could not afford to have sympathetic feelings towards the fairer sex. I was out a dollar plus cab fare. I went down to the concession counter in search of a coffee and a fried egg sandwich. There, sitting with the eternal grin on his homely features, was Ray Bestick. I remembered Ray principally not only for his never-failing good humour but because while at Heaton Park, during a 'spit and polish' parade, he had pulled out an outsize Meerschaum pipe and started smoking it.

Such a thing was unheard of, so utterly inconceivable, that no one noticed it.

He greeted me with a friendly blow to the chin and grinned like a happy dog.

'Well! You old bastard, how goes it?'

'Not bad, you fornicating old fart. What in hell brings you up from the sewers of *this* particular region?'

'Your good luck, I guess, Dixie. I'll let you buy my coffee.' He perched himself comfortably on a bar-stool. 'Perhaps,' he added, 'maybe my ability to fall on my feet had something to do with it.'

'You did mention something about falling. Did you have to bail out? The last time I saw you was at Manchester. Where did they post you?'

'Wait till the coffee comes, old man. I always seem to have a parched throat.'

'Small wonder, with that pot-bellied stove stuck in your kisser.'

'Could be,' he grinned, and after slaking the residual ashes located in his gullet, he proceeded to bring me up to date. 'I was sent to Pensacola, Dixie. I had stated a preference for fighter-pilot training. So where do the stunned clots send me? To flying-boat training. Me . . . and I can't even swim. But those waterbirds were bang-on kites, and I learned to fly. That's the main thing.'

'You're using the past tense?'

'That's right, Dixie. They dumped me.'

'And you don't care?'

'Not a damned bit. I have to agree with their assessment: "Not suited to command".'

'I suppose you'd better fill me in on the ghastly details.'

'Well,' he resumed after much slurping, 'on my last trip, I had a "sprog" instructor. New to the area and not as old as I was. As we went out to the boat together, he asked me if I'd got the flight plan and maps. "Right here, sir," I assured him, patting the wad of paperwork in my flying-boot. This instructor type kept eyeing me. I responded by a great show of confidence. You know, the spurious kind. Neither of us noticed a great threatening front was blowing in. I called up control, asked permission to take off, and got the usual crackling and static so I assumed we were free to go.

'There was a guy in a coast-guard cutter shining a green lamp at us. (When I was a kid, I had a flash-lamp for a birthday and couldn't stop flashing it till the battery was flat.) There was a fair amount of alto stratus, but I expected to break cloud at around 3,000. We didn't, but I pressed on. In these flying-boats, Dixie, the pilot and co-pilot sit side-by-side, and it could have been sort of chummy, but I couldn't get even a sideways smile out of this bod. He sat there with his jaw clamped. When I offered him some gum, he pushed it away without thanks. After about twenty miles, he enquired how much longer to the ETA new course. I told him I would look, so I pulled out what I thought was my map and flight plan. Instead, what do you think I pulled out? Now this'll kill you, Dixie: the current edition of *La Gaie Parisienne*! After a bit I found I was the only one laughing. The guy then wanted to know where I thought we were. Well, beyond the fact that we were heading out into the Atlantic, I hadn't too much of a clue. I said: "We'll be seeing Nantucket light soon, sir." He said he somehow doubted it, because we couldn't even see our wing-tips. "All along that coast, Dixie, the weather can clamp in pretty readily, and we had to faced up to the fact that we were up to our tonsils in a pea-soup fog. He told me to try the radio to see if we could get a wind vector. Nothing doing. I don't think there was a hell of a lot of juice in the battery."

'Why didn't you alter course and fly on the reciprocal?' I asked.

'Well, we did that, of course, Dixie, but right at the outset I couldn't quite remember what the original course was. You see, this bod was beginning to get to me, but eventually we were high-tailing it back the way we'd come. Well, you know what the chances are when you're in cloud and haven't a clue as to which way is home or which way is up, for that matter. Should we make a descent and hope to break cloud before we hit something? I suggested we stay put and orbit in a "rate one" turn. "Why?" the bod wanted to know. "Because it's possible someone has us plotted on a radar screen, then it's their job to get us down".'

'To cut a long story short, old boy, that's pretty well what happened. We continued orbiting with the radio on, but weak, and we did a lot of careful listening. We were eventually given a course to steer for a clear anchorage. It was calm water where we put down, but you would have pissed yourself with laughing. I landed her with the bloody floats up.'

'And the outcome was?'

'Oh, I caught the CO in a generous mood, and they're going to let me re-muster to air bomber. I had a few days to wait for the thing to be finalized, and I heard of a DC3 coming out to the Middle West so I hitched a ride. He's going back in half an hour, so I'd best be stirring.'

'And what about your "birdman" dreams? Don't you care?'

'Curiously enough, old boy, it doesn't bother me a bit. I know I'm a slap-happy type, and I wouldn't feel comfortable having a crew of some mothers' sons constantly depending on my own personal luck. I know I can fly with the best of them. I'm happy. And do you know something? A bombardier gets more pay than a pilot.'

'Oh yes, I know that. They get fourteen bob a day to a pilot's thirteen and sixpence. Well! well! well! This bombardier's job doesn't sound too bad a spec. You fly as second pilot and second navigator and also have a couple of Browning guns to fiddle with. That sounds all right.'

'It'll suit me, Dixie, if I don't make a balls of the course. If I said I'll keep in touch, that would be so much bullshit. I don't even write home, but it would be kinda all right by me if we flew together sometime.'

With that he shouldered his side-pack and made for the door. He didn't wave, but it took the room several minutes to get used to his absence.

What was it that little, piddling pedaller in the park had said? 'I guess a guy can do anything here, mister.' That being so, I was going to be the crackerjack of all pilots, and I was going to cut such a swath through the Huns that the turning-point of the war could be marked off from there. Just the same, that bombardier's position seemed to have a lot going for it.

This brought the week's leave to Friday, and Wacker Wright (who had favoured a USO hostel with his lively presence, on a sporadic basis) breezed in with a lovely piece of woman on his arm. He asked for a loan of a ten-spot. This was half of what I owned, but a Britisher cannot see a compatriot in distress without divvying up.

I told him I would be taking the night train back to Jackson City. He said: "Hang on, Dix. This bird has a car. We'll pick you up and run you to the depot.'

We took the long way around to the depot. Rosemary drove with natural freedom and expertise. I can see her now – short-sleeved arms impervious to the cooling slipstream of the silver convertible, clean golden hair streaming back from an untram-melled brow, chattering like a magpie over some inconsequen-tial drivel, finding it completely joyous and amusing. Rosemary: the clean, the carefree, the naive.

The train was waiting at the platform when we arrived.

'Go and grab yourself a seat, Dix,' said Wacker, 'or you'll probably finish up standing all night.'

So I went forward, dropped my cap on an empty seat, and then went back to say a last 'thanks' to the lucky youngsters. As the train moved out, I sauntered forward to my seat. As I finally reached my carriage and looked down its length, I was startled to see a crown of golden hair occupying the seat next to mine. I was to have a travelling companion. She did not look up as I assumed my seat.

'I hope you don't mind me sitting here,' she said softly.

'No, no, not at all. I was just a little surprised. The girl I was speaking to on the platform had hair just the same look as yours.'

'We probably go to the same beauty parlour. Was that your buddy she was with?'

'Yes, one of them.'

'And you've both been on leave?'

'Yes.'

'And he has found himself a nice girl? Well, better luck next time.'

'Look here! I don't know why you should assume I was looking for a girl. I happen to be married.'

'Well, goody for you. So am I.'

'Forgive me for saying so, but that seems a little bit unlikely. You don't look more than sixteen.'

Still looking ahead, she raised her hand which had been resting in her lap and covered by a cheap purse. She showed me a wedding ring (which did not have the appearance of being new) on the appropriate finger.

'I was married at fifteen,' she said.

'Where I come from, they think of marriage at sixteen as cradle-snatching.'

'Where I come from,' she mimicked, 'they think of it as respectable. How old were you when you got married?'

'Twenty-five.'

'And at twenty-seven, you're looking for a girl.'

'In my country, your remarks would be regarded as impertinent.'

'OK, OK, I'm sorry already. I must have misunderstood the look you were giving to that broad back on the platform there.'

'This conversation, young lady, has got ridiculous. Haven't you got a book or anything?'

'No, no books, no reading. Never formed the habit. The only book allowed in our house was the Bible, and when you get that as a steady diet, even Moses with all his magic gets a bit tiresome.'

'Why was that? Was your dad a parson or something?'

'No, but my mother was – and you know what they say: "The minister's kids are the brattiest kids on the block".'

'And are you a brat?'

'Well, I was, I guess. But like I told you, I'm married now.'

'So where is your husband?'

'OK. So now I have to produce my husband before I'm believed. It so happens he is in the Navy, and I am now on my way to join him.'

'You're shivering.'

'I'm not shivering. Shuddering some, maybe. So now you know where I'm going, how about coming clean about why you're cutting your leave short and scuttling back to base?'

Well, as we had the rest of the night in front of us and it was after all a nice, safe topic, I filled her in.

'You see, the dispatcher where I'm stationed, and her boyfriend who is my instructor, are trying to get me thrown off the course.'

'Tell them to work it . . . . Pardon me. That was not very lady-like observation, was it? The brat will keep surfacing. Yet I do feel where you are the underdog in the ring it's better to retreat than stand toe-to-toe and have your brains knocked out. Tell them you've reconsidered, and that you don't want to fly their lousy planes. They'll force you to continue. You'll see.'

'You know, you're delightfully amusing.'

'OK, but just don't call me amusingly delightful. It's too early in the evening for that kind of twaddle. If you are not

81

going back to base early to straighten out those lovebirds, what are your plans?'

'I'm not sure that I can explain it to you, but the type of plane I've been flying is totally different to the one I shall have to be dealing with in the next two months.'

'Like what? A plane is a plane, ain't it? Do you mean they're heavier and it takes more doing to keep them up in the sky?'

'No. The problem is conversion. Converting from one type of aircraft to another. For instance, the AT6 has a retractable under-cart; the Steerman's is fixed. It also has air-brakes, has selective gas tanks, radio transmitter and receiver, and a whole lot of things that I'm not used to. Now my idea is to spend a few hours on the deck in the cockpit of one of those birds so that I can select the right knob without thinking. Then when my instructor tries his fun-loving antics (as I know he will), I'll at least be able to have a fighting chance.'

She curled her nose. 'Nope,' she said, 'right from here I can recognize a losing hand. If those two lovers want you out, out you'll go. They'll make it a game, and when a game is played only one side can win. You are trump poor. I wouldn't play their game. And you know what? Somebody could get his ass killed. Pardon me.'

'Well, well! It's nice of you to be concerned, even if morbidly. How about you? Are you bubbling over with joy to be reunited with your husband?'

'Sure. Why not? Ain't that how it's supposed to be. Sure . . . sure.'

'I expect when a young couple have had to live apart for a while, there are some tricky little adjustments to be made – on his side as well as hers. It would be foolish to expect everything to be smooth sailing.'

'If you're planning to be doling out marital advice, Mister Man, just keep it. Everything's gonna be just great.'

'I'm delighted to hear it, but please don't call me Mister Man. I'm Arthur Day.'

'And I'm Jo Anne Kurie. Pleased to meet you. And if this darned train keeps sashaying around, we'll finish up being introduced good.'

Was this an invitation for what the Yanks called necking? I wasn't sure but I didn't think so. No, she was just another piece of flotsam, left insecure by the evil and upheaval of war and reaching for a friendly arm around the shoulder.

I drew her to me, and my shoulder seemed to provide a natural habitat for that clean, golden hair. The evening had given place to night.

'Go to sleep,' I said.

6

I arrived at Jackson City just as the civilian workers were
leaving for the airfield, so I was able to get a lift and soon I had
let myself into my barrack-room. I tip-toed through the eerie
stillness to my bed. There was a message stuck between the
blankets to the effect that there was a cable for me at the camp
post office. A dozen alarming reasons swarmed through my
brain to account for the fact that someone had sent me a cable.
I fairly shot around to the camp post office. The clerk was
locking the door. I made a futile plea.

'Come back at one o'clock, OK?' said the clerk.

I was, of course, furious but had to contain my fury until one
o'clock. When I got the buff envelope in my hand, I took three
deep breaths before I could nerve myself to open it. It was from
New York, handed in at the General Hospital Office. It read:

'Arthur - Stop - Larry - Admitted - HERE - Stop - Reason -
Peritonitis - Stop - Condition - Critical - Stop - Love - Miriam -
Stop.' Well, poor benighted Kratters. With the last of my pay,
I sent a return cable care of Doctor Kratz at New York
General, to read: 'Go for it, young Kratters. You can do it. See
you.'

On the way back from the post office, I passed the adjutant
who gave me a rather puzzled stare as if he couldn't quite
remember who I was.

After lunch, I sauntered down to the crew room, where they
were just pondering a new regulation which had come down
from the admin. office. It was to the effect that no unauthor-
ized student was to board any unoccupied aircraft. After
considering the matter, it seemed obvious that the adjutant
had remembered who I was, had read my mind, and had lost
no time in thwarting my intentions. It was all too apparent. I
had made no friend there, right from day one. Rather disconso-

late, I mooched around to the maintenance hangar to take in the scene from there. The thing that impressed me was the quiet calmness of the place and the sterile cleanliness. A number of fairly young women dressed in immaculate mechanics' overalls (from the turn-ups of which protruded fashionably spiked shoes) were going unhurriedly about their work: swarming into the aircraft, removing cowlings; exchanging altimeters, spark plugs, etc., with practised hand and eye. Each one had a gleaming set of mechanics' tools which no man could behold without contravening a commandment about covetousness all to hell.

As I watched, a young woman wearing a lovely blue bandana over her dark curls descended the steps from the storeroom. She was carrying a component of some kind and a sheaf of invoices or some such. Almost as she drew abreast to me, a gust of wind at the open door caught one of the papers and sent it skittering across the tarmac toward the flying field. My latent sprinting energy was rapidly on top, and I was soon restoring the errant paper to a suitably grateful young woman.

'If I had lost that 1046, I don't know what I'd have done,' she gasped, pushing her curls back into her headscarf.

She told me her name was Phyllis. And yes, it was a lovely day, and no, she didn't mind someone sitting in the front cockpit if she was working in the back. In fact, it would be handy to have someone up front when she was *changing rudder cables* and things like that.

It worked like a charm, and I was able to concentrate all my mental faculties on the imaginary flying of that aircraft, except when Phyllis' exotic perfume wafted through the cockpit to me and then slightly less so. One thing became apparent: I needed about as many arms and hands as an octopus to engage the many switches, pumps and levers that seemed to be demanded, more or less at the same time. Anyhow, at the end of the day, the AT6 had fewer mysteries and surprises than it hitherto had, and by the next day the rest of the lads started to dribble back. Many of them had been driven back from various corners of the continent by admirers and well-wishers, and fathers of well-wishers and admirers. What a country!

On the first day back on the course, we were introduced to advanced flying. Because of the problem of serviceability, there were only four AT6s on the line, a drastic reduction from the more than a dozen that were the usual complement. For that reason, students were allowed to solo with other students. Even with this economy, I went the whole week without getting airborne. Then a terrific amount of data was thrown at me on a catch-up basis. It was during this first week back that we suffered our first casualty. Farley had been paired up with Tiger Green, a laughing red-faced, American kid. They apparently spotted a haystack in a field and found that by swooping down they could spread that hay all over the field. But they made one swoop too many and the AT6 was spread over a good portion of that field; both students were killed.

We were assigned four students to an instructor, except in my case: I was Vinter's fifth. For nine days I didn't see the inside of an aircraft. Hallaway had been up solo twice. There was an unmistakable obstacle here, and I had to deal with it.

As I lay on my bunk that night, sleep wouldn't come. I thought of women. Specific women. I thought of Eve, at home expectant and confident: confident, when there we no reason on God's green earth for her confidence. Sweet, trusting Eve. Was I going to disappoint her? I thought of Miriam, a young woman alone in a seething, restless city, and her loving brother, critically ill, looking to her for a miracle. I thought of that poor girl-mother that I had met in the park. What would be the outcome of her sorry lot, I wondered. I thought of the girl in the train. Why had she shuddered at the thought of being reunited with her husband? So vulnerable, and yet so worldly wise. What had she said? 'Tell 'em to work it. Tell 'em you don't want to fly their lousy planes.' Well, I certainly would not go to a little sixteen-year-old bobbysoxer for advice. And yet, out of the mouths of babes . . . I had to bring the situation to a head. I jumped off the bed, switched on the desklight, and wrote an application to see the CO.

Squadron Leader Parke was a tall, pallid man with grey, unblinking eyes. Of indeterminate age, he was of most determinable nationality – so painfully British, the enemy of excitement and emotion. Everything had to be boiled down into slow, deliberate understatement. He glanced down at my application and appeared to give it respectful thought, and after a few sporadic questions he got down to the meat of the matter.

'You say you're not getting enough flying in to make you

perform well in the air?'

'That's right, sir.'

'Well, you know, Day, we are experiencing something of a problem with regard to the serviceability of the aircraft. At the moment, I think we only have two airworthy AT6s on the line. Things change from time to time and all we can do is hope more flying time can come your way. Er, is this all?'

'Well, no sir. I was wondering if you would consider allowing me to re-muster to air-bomber.'

'Air-bomber? If I get an application from you in writing, I'll deal with it.'

'I would rather be a first-class bombardier than a failed pilot.'

'The possibility of your failing has not been presented yet. If during the course you haven't showed up well, owing to lack of air experience, due allowance will be made to you on your final exam.'

'Thank you, sir. Let's hope Jerry will make suitable allowance also.'

He fixed me with a steely glare. 'You may return to the flights,' he said.

He was down on the flights bright and early next morning, and I heard my name called. The CO fell into step beside me as I went out to the aircraft and wordlessly climbed into the rear compartment. When I had made a preliminary inspection of the exterior, I climbed into the front. I waggled the controls and watched the rudder and ailerons respond, and I then carried out a normal but careful cockpit check. Holding the stick firmly between my knees and generating the starter gyro, I yelled 'Clear!' and switched the ignition to On. I didn't think she was going to catch, at first, but then with a rather apologetic cough she sprang alive. Having crossed that hurdle, I tried my luck with the still unfamiliar radio. The tower seemed interested in what I was doing and where I intended to go; after having also crossed that hurdle I was soon roaring across the airfield in great style.

'I want you to climb north out of the circuit,' the CO commanded, 'and flatten out at about eight thou'.'

'Very good, sir.'

It was a fair morning with about four-tenths cirro-stratus and no wind to speak of.

'Let's try a couple of Lazy Eights,' I was instructed. They came out well.

'Now, can you do me a Himmelmann?'

'I can try, sir.' That also went well.

'I want you just to fly me around, ad lib for the next twelve minutes and then take me back.'

So that was it. I joined traffic perfectly and made a smooth 'pancake' landing. As we climbed out of the cockpit, I suppose the 'old man' thought he had to make some comment.

'When you change to reserve tank,' he said, 'when you're on your downwind leg, make perfectly sure that lever has gone over with a clunk or you may find you're landing on some awfully thin air . . . .'

'How did it go?' Wacker later wanted to know.

'Bang on! No complaints.'

'Did he ask for your logbook?'

'No.'

'Good. Oh, they say if he's gonna ground you, he always asks for your logbook. I'd say you're in, Dixie, you lucky old bastard.'

I was more than moderately elated. I had taken the initiative. I had confronted a tricky situation, head-on, and it had worked. The approval of the CO, with only another six weeks to go to the end of the course, was tantamount to a passing grade on the final. I went back to the billet and wrote to Eve. I would post it tomorrow. I noticed on the bulletin board that I was down for night flying that night, not a delightful prospect in dusty July on a bumpy, remote landing-field.

Vinter was even more remote than the field and scarcely commented as we went through the tiresome routine of circuits and bumps. By one a.m. the air was even dustier. The night was very dark, and the lights of the landing-strip were scarcely distinguishable from the lights of the planes awaiting takeoff. I hate confusion, and confusion reigned. Nothing could be seen clearly, and the deafening roar of those Continental radial engines made hearing out of the question. At that time, the instructors went into a huddle, and Vinter came striding over to me. 'Hop into the back,' he said. 'We're returning to base.'

I had been flying from the front seat, but I was too tired to argue. As he strapped himself in, he picked up my flying helmet which I had left on the dash, and then noticing that it wasn't his, he hung it on a little hook at the side of the windshield. He was obviously in a desperate hurry to get home. He bustled to the front of the waiting line of returning aircraft and soon had us bounced into the homeward stretch. On our arrival at the airfield, instead of coming to a stop and then taxiing around the perimeter, Vinter kept the throttle half-open and roared across the field in the direction of the HQ block. I knew immediately what the score was. He had put a call through to Betty. Then came the crash.

Crashes do seem to have some far-reaching effects on people, the course of subsequent events, and things. This one was to have.

First came the noise. It was like a huge thrashing machine going into action. A hail of a thousand particles of debris showered us. The aircraft moved tail-high and thrust its nose into whatever it was we'd hit. We had been taxiing with the canopy open, but as we tipped forward the canopy slid closed with a crash. Vinter killed the engine and managed to get the canopy open enough for him to squeeze out and slide to the ground. I heaved on my part of the canopy, but it had jammed. I was, however, able to get some movement by rocking it from side to side. At last, with a supreme effort, I was able to get one shoulder through the gap and, shrugging free of the entangling harness, I somersaulted to the burning turf, gratefully leaving my flying gear to the eager flames. I could hear a hissing, and I knew the tank would be next. Vinter still stood there, mesmerized by the colourful display. I moved back twenty yards or so; if he wanted a front, close view, let him. He hadn't stirred himself to free me from the cockpit. He staggered back, holding his forehead. By now the countryside for miles around was bathed in a wonderful glow of fiery light, and soon a sizeable crowd had collected to view the last rites of what had once been a flying-machine. What we had collided with was the wind tee (a slope-sided, plywood structure set out a little way into the airfield from the duty pilots' hut). And so eventually to bed.

Vinter became an overnight celebrity, a kind of air hero. The local radio station gave a full account of how one of Mr Vinter's students had misjudged his approach and had over-shot the landing area and completely destroyed the aircraft and wind tee. Vinter was striding about the crew room,

grinning broadly, with a huge wad of discoloured surgical gauze taped to his left cheek.

'Well, I guess that's flying,' he laughed. 'Yes sir, that's flying.'

I was required to go to Headquarters. The orderly-room clerk handed me a form, in triplicate, for my signature.

'What am I signing?' I wanted to know.

'An accident report.'

'Then why is there all this blank space above where you've marked your cross?'

'That's where I'll be typing in an account of the accident. Uncle Sam has let you have one of his kites to burn, for cripes sake. Do you argue about letting him have a receipt?'

I took the form and wrote: 'At approximately one a.m. on 12 July, 1941, while I was a student passenger, my instructor M. Vinter collided said aircraft with an unlighted obstacle, resulting in the complete demolition of both. (Signed) A. Day, 163726.'

'You'll never get away with it,' the clerk assured me as I left.

That same afternoon, I was ordered to the CO's office and told to wait outside the door. It had been left ajar, purposely I suppose. There sounded to be several people there already. The adjutant for one, and Wilbur Nye's voice I could recognize, and then there was the CO. He was commenting: 'There's bound to be one hell of a stink at command about this. We're losing more kites than Bomber Command.'

Wilbur Nye apparently thought this was really funny. His laughter was loud and lingering. The Station Commander asked: 'Have we got the instructor's report here. [There was the sound of papers being shuffled.] Hm. Hm. I see . . . . Sound type, is he, eh?'

'Oh, splendid type. Excellent flyer,' said the adjutant's voice.

'One of the safest men you could have around. Why that guy just about wrote a book on safety, but no instructor's safe when a student can write off a ship like that right in front of your very eyes.' This was Wilbur's contribution.

'There is this conflict of account. This diametrically opposed version. Are we positive who was at the controls?'

'Well, sir, with regard to that, Day's helmet and goggles [or rather the identifiable remains of Day's helmet and goggles] were found in the front cockpit. Need I say more?'

'I see what you mean. Oh, very well then. We'd better get him in.'

The adjutant opened the door and called me in. The station commander sat there with a wintry look.

'Day, it's my decision to terminate your training. I don't suppose this comes as a surprise to you. This is the second accident you've had, and we can't afford to risk a third. You will be sent from here to Toronto, where they will decide your future for you. It is my recommendation that you stay as far from aircraft as possible.'

'You have seen my report, sir?'

'Yes, I have it in front of me. Unfortunately for you, there is absolutely no corroboration for it, and it is totally at variance with the only witness, that is your instructor. I must say this outcome of your training has come as something of a surprise to me. I wish you good luck in whatever branch of the service you eventually find yourself. This is Tuesday. Have your kit ready to board Thursday's train. Dismissed.'

Wacker was almost emotionally moved. 'Hard Cheddar, Dixie, old horse. I'd shove an umbrella up Vinter's arse and then open it. But Dixie, don't for cripes sake *do* anything. You could finish up worse off than you are.'

'Oh yes? How?'

I went back to the billet and tore up the letter that I'd written the day before to Eve. Phyllis was sympathetic, though of course she had no conception of the enormity of my misfortune.

'Sure am sorry. Sure you're bound to feel depressed and blue. No, I don't mind you sitting in the cockpit while I work.'

For months I had vividly anticipated our departure from Jackson City. There would be cheering and jeering, hoots of laughter, singing and joking. Well, half-a-dozen chaps did come down to the depot to see me off, Wacker among them.

'So long, Dix. Remember, *no bono carborundum*. That is, don't let the bastards wear you down. I'm glad you didn't *try* anything.'

I didn't hear about the accident until months later. I found an old copy of the *Oklahoma Times* and it referred briefly to it: 'Flying instructor's second crash fatal . . . . While testing an aircraft today, M. Vinter flew too low and became impaled in the trees east of the perimeter track. He and his passenger, Mrs E. Gorski, were killed instantly. Vinter had previously been cautioned against low-flying aerobatics.'

I arrived at the exhibition ground in Toronto, then known as Number 1 Manning Depot, in the middle of July, having stopped off briefly in Chicago in order to shed some of my feelings of hurt and misuse. We were paraded (myself and 200 others who had fallen foul of Yankee instruction) in a vast parade-ground previously used for the marshalling of animals. Standing there was tedious in the extreme, so when the warrant officer called for volunteers for a temporary writing assignment, I took the necessary two paces forward.

'OK, you report to Sergeant Mansfield in the re-board office.'

And off I went. Sergeant J.A. Mansfield was a clean-cut, clear-headed man of thirty. His level grey eyes saw, and he was informed. He looked up from his desk as I entered, and his hand reached out to a pile of documents.

'These,' he said, 'are a pile of AMOs. Can you file them into an order so that they can be cross-referenced not only from the title but from the information contained and set up an index? The writing doesn't have to be special, as the corporal will type it out afterwards.'

'Yes, Sergeant.'

'You can? Very good. There's a desk over there. Go to it.'

So began my brief clerical career. From 8 a.m. to 4.30 p.m. it was a man's world, that office: crisp and businesslike. Telephone conversations were clear, factual and brief, as was all other business. The second day I was there, I tackled the corporal about Mansfield.

'Is he for real?'

'You're goldarned right he's for real. He's the smartest cookie the UK has ever sent over here. Works like a horse but always has a good reserve, if you know what I mean. He used to be a fairly big shot in Fleet Street before the war. Ran a weekly column of his own: lithography, handwriting, that sort of stuff.'

At 4.30 on the fourth day, I was just finishing up a lengthy entry and hadn't noticed the time. It had gone quiet, everyone having drifted away.

'It's 4.30,' called Mansfield across the office.

'Yes, Sergeant. I'm on my way.'

'How is it working out?'

'OK, Sergeant. Should have it finished by tomorrow.'

'Fetch over what you've done, and let me take a look.'

I took over my work and watched his eyes narrow as he followed the thing through stage to stage, without comment. Then he reached out his lanky leg and hooked his foot into a nearby chair and propelled it to me.

'Take a pew,' he said.

I sat and watched as he leafed quickly and critically through the pile. Then he laid it on the desk and strode over to the filing cabinet. He extracted a file and returned to the desk, pinching his chin thoughtfully.

'Any idea what I'm doing?'

'Puzzling over something, maybe.'

'And how!'

He straightened up in his chair and looked at me earnestly.

'I have your documents here,' he said, 'including a report on you from Jackson City. I expect now and then to have a factor of variance in the print-out of a subject, but none of this stuff adds up. I'm comparing the characteristics in your handwriting and what the Yanks have to say on you. What happened down there in the States?'

I gave him a brief resumé. 'Does it matter, Sarge? I played a losing hand, that's all. Someone has to.'

'I agree. There's nothing anyone can do to reverse the verdict of this report. Our dealings with the Americans will always be on the sensitive side, and no Britisher is going to cast doubts on their integrity and judgement and make it stick. I couldn't. I wouldn't. What I can do, if you like, is get a re-board hearing. How would a bombardier's course appeal to you? You'd go for that, eh? Well, all I can do is get you an interview. The rest is up to you. Think carefully about it; it could be important.'

The next day, sixteen airmen were interrogated and their future roles decided on. At the close of the session, when the hands of the clock were converging on quitting time, the re-board officer looked over to Mansfield.

'Is that all, Sergeant?'

'There is one more case, sir. Our cadet, Day, has asked to see you, sir. His application is here. Day, will you come this way?'

94

There was nothing but factual respect in the words the NCO used, but they managed to convey a whole wealth of goodwill and approbation.

The re-board officer glanced up at me kindly. 'Stand at ease. So the piloting didn't work. So you'd like to take a stab at bombing . . . . That it?'

'Well, sir, I do think more consideration must be given to bombing. To go over enemy territory and drop bombs is in itself an achievement, sir, but emptying a few tons of TNT into a German field and frightening a few German cows isn't going to win us the war quickly.'

'Go on.'

'I feel the situation needs the services of airmen who have come to know aircraft thoroughly. The attitude of the aircraft at the time of the bombs' release is critical. I think it takes a man of maturity to arrange it so.'

'And do you consider yourself to be mature?'

'With respect, sir, I'm sure I am more mature now, sir, than I once was.'

The OC re-board chuckled. 'I'm allowing your application,' he said.

7

Thirty years later, I was taking the evening stroll across the Park to the Albert Hall. It was a mild evening, on the whole, with only occasional swirls of more chilling air, children of some vagrant air mass.

It had been the kind of a day – parts to relish and enjoy; parts to tweak my ego; and some which struck a vague, eerie, discordant note, bits of a jigsaw that would not fit or go away.

Life was somehow like that, I mused, as I watched the darkening sky ahead; I could sense, rather than see, the glowing fluorescent signs behind me, making the world aware of the Park Lane and Grosvenor House Hotels. You won some, and you lost some, and the eerie fitful chills that went with you through the quietening evening were all part of the day.

Soon looming before me was the Albert Memorial, a fitting memorial to royal love, and a reminder that however exalted may be our rank or station, the final enemy has to be faced.

With sombre mood I allowed my footsteps to lead me to that unique volume of sound which was the Royal Albert Hall. I saw my daughter's name decorously displayed on the small billboards in the front of the building, with diagonal stripes across the front: PENELOPE DAY, TONIGHT.

'A wonderful house tonight, sir,' mentioned Pickens, the doorman, as I strode past him along the passage to the stars dressing-room. My watch told me there was just a quarter of an hour to go before the finale. I sank down into one of those low, upholstered chairs to wait. I then became aware of an uncertain footstep outside the door.

'Come in, come in,' I called. 'You can wait inside.' Reporters, celebrities and journalists were the usual run, and it was difficult at all times to tell one from the other. The door was eased open by a big, grey American, middle-aged and solid. He tapped the side of his leg with a rolled-up newspaper as he advanced into the room.

'Hello,' I said. 'My daughter will be down very soon.'

'Thank you. Then you must be the father of Penelope Day?'

'Yes.'

'Ex-Squadron Leader Day, part of the Dam-Buster force, and inventor of the Mark three-zero bomb sight?'

'Well, yes. You seem to be extraordinarily informed for a newspaper man, and I do take you to be that.'

'You're now retired, and living on a house-boat up in the Putney area, having one child, a daughter. Your wife was killed in the blitz?'

'More or less correct, but my wife died in childbirth while I was serving overseas. May I ask why this remarkable interest?'

'You may, sir, you may indeed. Let me tell you. I was the sheriff's assistant back in 1942. They were days when a lot of things happened, and people couldn't seem to stop and think about any particular thing. Exciting, breathtaking things were happening all over hell's half-acre, you might say. No-one was going to pay too much attention to a little trainer plane biting the dust, and down there in Jackson County we were no better than the rest. Things were not right, though, about that little crash. Why, that pilot could fly the ass of anything flyable. Why was this particular little bird not flyable? These things happen, we know, but the element of doubt is a nagging thing. Yes sir, a nasty, nagging thing. The relations between the Allies and Uncle Sam at that time were kinda strong, yet delicate, and when I suggested that we invite a certain airman to return to the States in case he was able to throw a light on this puzzle, nobody busted their jeans to get it done.'

'And what was the outcome?'

'Well, rightly speaking, there weren't no outcome. People just got concerned with other things. The file now is getting yellow with age, but I've always been curious about how that young airman turned out. You know, the one we might have interrogated. Was he musical at all? Did he think back to those last two days in Jackson City and wonder if everything was shipshape?'

The American had not taken the seat which I indicated but gently strode up and down that small room, his head back, his eyes half-closed, making an obvious effort at complete recall.

97

These bloody Yanks could be relied on to make a five-star production out of everything.

'We were short, all the time, of one last positive link to make that cosy little crash into a murder. And murder it was. Experience tells me that the perpetrator always likes to leave a little clue behind to prove he was no coward. This man was no different. Just inside the hangar wall where that AT6 had been serviced, were three peculiar marks which no-one could explain or account for. Three oval marks, almost side-by-side. Yes sir.'

Now he sank down into one of the chairs, and laying his newspaper down beside him, he produced a luxurious cigar and went about getting it into operation. Apparently, he relied heavily on the dramatic effect of billowing clouds of smoke soaring upwards.

'Three years,' he said, 'after the expiry of the statute of limitations. I knew for sure what those marks were. I was thumbing through old wartime songs and the last one was by your Vera Lynn. Suddenly I recognized the marks that I'd seen on that hangar wall. They were notes of music. Above the musical notes were the end of the lyric *There'll come another day*. It was perhaps the clumsy signature, but who could make *An Arthur Day* more plain? Well sir, just for the matter of interest, I thought I'd drop in, as part of my vacation, and let you know that perfect crimes do not come that easy.' With that he shrugged deeper into his raincoat and walked through the door.

I felt chilled, shaken and sick. Not remorseful, mind you. Those damned 'bedmates' had deliberately arranged themselves across my war. Vinter had, without moving a muscle, watched me trapped and struggling in an aircraft that he had fired. Even after all those years I was satisfied and felt favoured by fates that I had been allowed to fight back so effectively. No, it was the thought of the wonderful years of respect that I had enjoyed since I had put all that on the line.

I sprawled there, shaken. My eyes drifted over to the newspaper that the Yank had left behind. It was the British edition of the *Kansas Herald*. In the right-hand column was the photo of a young army air corps captain who had been killed that week in Vietnam. *What was there about that photo?* What was there about that face? Those slightly hooded eyes. *Who did they*

remind me of? Those questioning brows. The caption beneath the picture merely read Captain *Ewing Destry*, aged twenty-nine . . . .

I knew I was looking at the picture of my son.